Regression to the Mean

A Novel of Evaluation Politics

For W,

In honor of our mutual friend.

Eric

2003

Regression to the Mean

A Novel of Evaluation Politics

by
Ernest R. House

Information Age Publishing, Inc.
Charlotte, North Carolina • www.infoagepub.com

This is a work of fiction. All the characters and events portrayed in this book are fictional, and any resemblance to real people or incidents is purely coincidental.

Library of Congress Cataloging-in-Publication Data

House, Ernest R.
 Regression to the mean : a novel of evaluation politics / by Ernest R. House.
   p. cm.
 ISBN-13: 978-1-59311-849-5 (pbk.)
 ISBN-13: 978-1-59311-850-1 (hardcover)
 1. Educational evaluation--Political aspects--Fiction. 2. Educational evaluation--Moral and ethical aspects--Fiction. I. Title.
 PS3608.O863R45 2008
 813'.6--dc22

                                                                               2007037773

ISBN 13: 978-1-59311-849-5 (pbk.)
       978-1-59311-850-1 (hardcover)
ISBN 10: 1-59311-849-X (pbk.)
       1-59311-850-3 (hardcover)

Copyright © 2007 IAP–Information Age Publishing, Inc.

All rights reserved. No part of this publication may be reproduced, stored in a retrieval system, or transmitted, in any form or by any means, electronic, mechanical, photocopying, microfilming, recording or otherwise, without written permission from the publisher.

Printed in the United States of America

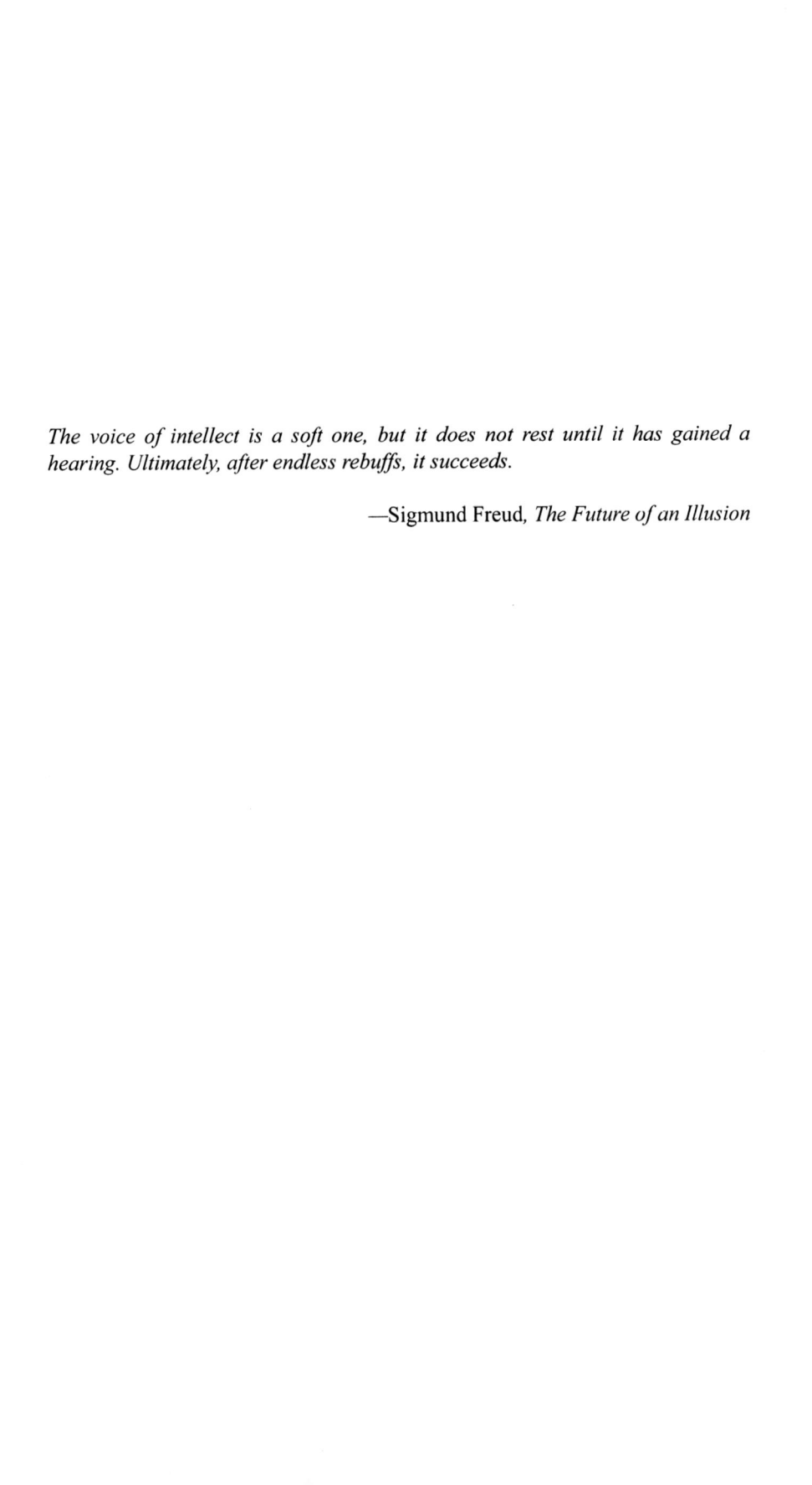

The voice of intellect is a soft one, but it does not rest until it has gained a hearing. Ultimately, after endless rebuffs, it succeeds.

—Sigmund Freud, *The Future of an Illusion*

CHAPTER ONE

Looking out across the cornfields from his office window, Reeder wondered how he had gotten himself into such a place. Across the campus the fields stretched into the distance as far as he could see. And it would be winter before long. Bleak. Fit his mood. He turned back to the yellow note pad and rested his chin on his fists. Where was he? He began to read his uneven scrawl again. The phone rang.

"This is the Mayor's office, New York City." A woman's voice. How old was she?

"This is Velma Williams, with Mayor Kuhnsmiller's office. We have a project you might be interested in."

How did they get his name, a thousand miles away? She began to explain. It was complicated.

"The New York school system has a new head. He's called a Chancellor, not a superintendent, as in most places." Just like New York City. A bit grandiose, he thought. But what the hell, they could hardly compete with university administrators.

"The Chancellor, Richard Pellegrini, has instituted a new policy. If students don't get a certain score on the citywide test, they can't go on to the next grade level. They are held back for the next year until they do get a passing score. They flunk."

He took a sip from his coffee cup. Yuck, the coffee was cold. It was bad enough when it was hot. Like this it was poison. The director of the center insisted on making the coffee in a big urn, and the stuff tasted metallic. Since the director was in the office in the morning long before anyone else and made the coffee, it was difficult to complain.

"What if the kids don't achieve the score the next year?" he asked.

"They fail again, until they do get the right score. It's called the Second Chance program."

Sounds like more Last Chance, Reeder thought as he waved a student away from his door, indicating he was on the phone. He recognized the mentality. Toughen up, crack down. Politicians had tried it for drugs, crime, welfare, the homeless, you name it. A fix-it-all solution for things they didn't want to spend money on. Trouble was, it never worked. But he was paid to evaluate, not preach.

She went on before he could say anything. An earthy voice. What did she look like?

"You see, Pellegrini grew up in a tough part of the city, a poor Italian neighborhood. And he made it out. He's been very successful. So he figures others should be able to make it too. He thinks teachers and students are not trying hard enough. If he clamps down on them, they will perform better. Too much slack in the system. The teachers give up and the kids give up. Everybody takes it easy. The teachers get by but the kids pay the price."

He remembered seeing a newspaper photo of Pellegrini. A fat guy with not much hair. Evidently, the tough discipline didn't apply to the Chancellor himself. He looked a little like LaGuardia, the Mayor from the 1940s. Perhaps New Yorkers were fat because there wasn't any place to exercise. They loaded up on pastrami sandwiches at the deli and took taxis everywhere.

Reeder turned his chair back towards the window and looked out across the flat Midwestern plains. Not a hill in sight.

"So you want me to evaluate the program," he said.

"No, no," she said. "Well, not exactly. We want you to *oversee* the evaluation. You see, New York has an unusual financial arrangement. You remember years ago when the city went bankrupt?"

He remembered. There had been lots of media coverage, and a Wall Street financier had been brought in to straighten out the city budget. The plan worked, more or less. The city got back on its feet.

"Yes, right, I remember." It had been a while.

"Well, in that reorganization of the city government, the deal was that the Mayor's office would provide half the school budget. We have a say in how the money on schools is spent."

"Right. Most school districts have their own financing, separate from the city government. Part of the progressive reforms." He figured she knew this or didn't care, but he wanted to say something to show that he had some knowledge of the issues, peripheral though it might be.

"Well, some people on the Mayor's staff think this new program will cost a lot of money and that it won't work. This year the district failed twenty-five thousand students. All those students have to go to summer school, which costs extra. Plenty extra." She paused. Was there someone else listening on her end?

"The students that don't achieve high enough test scores at the end of summer have to repeat the same grade they were in before. And the district has promised small classes of no more than eighteen for these students. Which means this year alone they had to hire nine hundred more teachers to staff the extra classes. A lot of money. Ninety million dollars. That has to come from the Mayor's budget."

"Why don't you just tell them no? Don't do the program."

"Well," she paused again. "The Chancellor is close to the Mayor personally and appealed to him. So the Mayor said let's try it. We fell back on insisting that the program be evaluated so we know whether it works. If not, it's over. Dead. That's the deal."

"But you don't want me to evaluate it?"

"No, when we insisted on an evaluation, the Chancellor's office said, 'Ok. We have a staff of sixty people who evaluate programs. Our staff can do the job.' That's when we came up with the idea of someone overseeing the evaluation. We don't have the expertise to know if the evaluation the district does is any good. And, frankly, we don't trust them entirely. We need someone to tell us if the evaluation is ok."

"Why me? I'm a thousand miles away. You can find someone closer. New York is a big place."

"When we decided to do it this way, with the monitoring, we asked around the country for names of people who could do the job. This isn't going to be easy, dealing with these city agencies. We need someone tough enough for the job. Your name came up most often. We thought we would talk to you first to see if you are interested."

That almost sealed the deal. Reeder was flattered to hear his name mentioned like this. That others thought he was tough. The project sounded interesting. Political dynamite. High profile. Filled with confrontation, no doubt. The way he liked it. It had been a while since he had been in a situation like this. He needed face-to-face conflict to jar him from the routines of academic life. The endless talk in faculty meetings could turn gold into lead.

"Ok," he said. "Why don't you send me some information about the program and how the oversight will work. I'll think about it and come up with some ideas."

Reeder finished discussing details with the Mayor's assistant, hung up the phone, and settled back in his chair. He wondered what he had gotten himself into. This was a world he knew nothing about. Maybe it was more than he could handle. He looked out the window at the flat land again. What the hell. At least it would get him out of the cornfields for a while.

CHAPTER TWO

A week later Reeder got another unexpected call. This time it was from the United Parents Federation, the parent union in New York. A man's voice.

"Professor Reeder, when you come to New York City to visit the Mayor's office, we would like to talk to you. We represent three hundred fifty thousand parents, and we think the Second Chance program has serious problems. We are not in favor of it. We are doing our own evaluation."

Reeder was surprised at the call and unsure how to respond. He had little understanding about his role with the Mayor's office. Here was another party intruding already. He stalled by asking for information.

"What don't you like about the program?"

"The program penalizes minorities. Elementary classes in the city have forty-two students in them. Eighty percent of these students are from minority backgrounds. Mostly African Americans and Latinos. Many don't speak English. Which students do you think fail when they give the tests?"

"But when they fail, they get extra help," Reeder said. "Maybe that's help they need to succeed." The man's voice sounded as if he could be African American. Hard to tell. He was probably right about the minorities, Reeder figured. It would be the minorities who were failing. And they would be the ones held back in school. But he didn't want to concede this point until he could figure things out. The man went on.

"We don't think this program works, even with small classes and extra help. It's discriminatory."

"Why don't you present your views to the school administration?"

"We have tried and tried. They don't listen. We are frozen out. They don't care what we think. They've made that clear. They listen to no one outside their little inner group. A closed circle. They think they know best. We're just angry parents to them."

"Well, three hundred fifty thousand parents is a lot of people, even in New York. They must hear something."

Reeder guessed the setup. A group as large as the parents union was too big for members to be active, other than paying dues. The union would be a tiny part of their lives, something parents belonged to because it was a good thing. That meant a staff ran the organization. The district administrators could write off the union staff as professional troublemakers who didn't have the kids' interest at heart. Do-gooders or interested in promoting their own careers.

"That's why we are going to do an evaluation of our own, to show the program is not working."

"How are you going to do that?"

"We are going to interview parents and students."

So they believed they could conduct a study based on what they learned in a social science course, Reeder thought. It wasn't that simple. Amateur evaluations had little influence. Still, it was interesting they were going to attempt their own study. Something to keep in mind.

Reeder decided to quit stalling. There wasn't much he could do with the man other than swap opinions. Nonproductive until he discovered more about the program.

"I really haven't heard anything about a trip to New York, so it's premature to plan on meeting you. I have to work out the project details with the people there first."

"Oh, you are coming to New York a week from Thursday. To meet with people in the Mayor's office and the Chancellor's office."

"Well, I haven't heard anything about it," Reeder said, off stride. The information surprised him. Was the man right? To get him off the phone, Reeder said he would meet with the union after he had worked out an agreement with the Mayor and Chancellor. The man accepted the assurance.

Late that afternoon, Reeder received another phone call. From the Chancellor's office. Come to the city a week from Thursday. The union knew about his plans before he did. Hello, New York.

CHAPTER THREE

No matter how many times Reeder flew into New York, he was impressed with the skyline. The skyscrapers were not that much bigger than in Chicago or other cities. There were just so many of them. As the plane dipped slowly on its guide path in, he could see miles and miles of buildings, not just a cluster or two. Now, in the twilight, the buildings were lit up, which enhanced their mystery.

The school district contact had told him the administrators wanted to talk to him at the central offices in Brooklyn before he went to the Mayor's office the next morning. It was dark, nearly 8 o'clock, before his taxi arrived at 110 Livingston Street. The building looked deserted. He checked through the security guard, who was expecting him, and took the elevator to the top floor, the Chancellor's offices.

The Deputy Chancellor's office was dimly lit. He could see the lights of Manhattan skyscrapers in the background. Six men were waiting for him. A large African American man got up to shake his hand.

"Good to meet you. I am Sam Kepner."

Kepner was assistant Chancellor, the man Reeder had made arrangements with over the phone. Reeder had never met him but he knew his name. Kepner had spent years in Washington before coming to New York. The man had a good reputation. He seemed affable enough.

The second man was the Deputy Chancellor, George Clough. He was tall, thin, stiff. Not so friendly. Probably the hatchet man.

Two men were in charge of departments, and the other two assistants. As Reeder shook their hands, Kepner motioned him to a chair against the wall. The six men sat down in a semicircle facing him.

"How was your flight?"

"Ok. A little bumpy coming in."

"Did you have any trouble getting in from the airport?"

"No, just some traffic at this time of evening." He felt tense, considering how the men were arrayed in front of him.

"Tomorrow you are going to meet with people from the Mayor's office. What we want you to understand tonight is who is paying you."

Kepner paused for a few moments to let his comment sink in.

"Although the Mayor's office chose you for the job, the money to pay you is coming from the school district. We are your employer. You understand that?" The way he said it was a command as much as a question.

He paused again. It was difficult for Reeder to read the expressions of the six men in the dim light. He sensed they were not friendly.

"You understand that?"

Kepner was waiting for a response.

Reeder hesitated. Until now he thought he was working for the Mayor. Clearly, the district had a different idea of who was in charge. He wondered if the Mayor's office had the same understanding. He would have to sort this out. But not here, not now.

"Yes, I understand that."

Reeder knew the money was coming from the school district. But it was coming at the insistence of the Mayor. Of course, Kepner was saying something else. He was saying who was boss. What Reeder didn't say was that he did not agree that who paid the bills called the shots, as they seemed to think.

"How much will your budget be?" Clough, the Deputy Chancellor, entered the discussion for the first time.

"It depends what your evaluation consists of," Reeder said. "I haven't seen the evaluation plan."

The small nervous man in the navy blazer spoke.

"Essentially, we are collecting test scores for the students involved in the program and analyzing those. That's the evaluation in a nutshell."

Reeder figured this must be the head of the evaluation department, Rick Cole. He hadn't been able to keep their names straight after the introductions.

"Just test scores? Nothing else?" Reeder said. "Isn't that a little risky? It's pretty difficult to get gains on standardized tests. Hard to do. You might be setting the program up for failure."

"We are getting good gains already. Impressive gains. Besides, that's all anyone in this city is interested in, the test scores. So that is what we are giving them."

"If I were designing the evaluation, I would collect other kinds of information to balance off the tests."

"As I said, test scores are what people in New York are interested in. It wouldn't make any difference what the other information was. And the program results have been impressive so far."

So this is a one-ring circus, Reeder thought. He had given them his best advice about collecting other information. If that was what they wanted to do, ok. Their attitude was typical. Sponsors of new programs always thought their programs would raise test scores. Maybe they had to think that way to have the guts to try something new. But test scores were difficult to increase—unless you taught the test to the students. You could do it that way.

"You're doing all the data collection and analysis?"

"Right. The district—my office—collects the test data, and we analyze the scores. Then we publish reports on the program based on the results. The reports are public information."

The man was staking out his territory. To Reeder, maybe to the others. Probably a good move on his part.

"If we have access to the data and don't have to collect information ourselves, we can audit the evaluation for about seventy thousand dollars a year." Reeder dropped a number he had thought about on the plane.

"Jesus, that's a lot of money for simply looking over our shoulder!"

Kepner came back to life at the mention of money.

"Well, we need to make trips out here to check things out, maybe redo some of the data analyses. That budget would include our travel."

Reeder thought the budget was on the light side but figured he could get more from the district if needed, given the circumstances. If he lasted that long. It was difficult to estimate costs when you were unclear what the tasks were. Auditing someone else's evaluation was not the way things were done ordinarily.

"I can send you a budget when I get back. It could cost less."

There was no sense making this project a university contract. The university would take months to process the proposal and add a huge overhead to the budget costs. It was not set up to handle projects like this.

Kepner looked at Clough, the Deputy. No discernible sign passed between them but Kepner said, "Ok, we can do that. We do need a detailed budget of estimated costs. We hold the money. You submit your claims to us for work completed."

"Well, as detailed as I can make it. I am guessing at what we are going to do."

"One page will be enough."

Three men had not said anything. Reeder guessed that the three doing the talking were the ones he had to deal with. And the Chancellor, wherever he was. No sign of him.

It was getting late. The men had spent a long day and were squirming in their chairs. Kepner suggested they quit and that Reeder take a taxi to his hotel in Manhattan. This neighborhood was no place to walk around this time of night. Reeder flagged a taxi at the door of the building while the security guard watched.

Manhattan was spectacular in the evening as the taxi arched across Brooklyn Bridge through traffic. The school district office was at one foot of the bridge and the Mayor's office at the other. As he crossed over the massive structure, Reeder remembered Hart Crane's poem about the bridge.

> "How many dawns, chill from his rippling rest
> The seagull's wings shall dip and pivot him,
> Shedding white rings of tumult, building high
> Over the chained bay waters Liberty—"

By chance, Crane wrote the poem in the same room from which the paralyzed engineer who built the bridge supervised its construction. Funny how things worked out. They reached the other side of the East River and entered Manhattan.

CHAPTER FOUR

As he shaved next morning in his hotel room, Reeder listened to the television news. The Mayor of New York was on, standing in front of an elementary school. Reeder looked around the corner to listen.

"I have raised the test scores in New York City," the Mayor said.

He was referring to the Second Chance program. The television spot was a political advertisement. Slick. The Mayor was running for office again, and the schools were a central issue in the campaign apparently. The retention program was the main educational reform. According to the Mayor, it was a great success. It looked as if the Mayor wanted more than higher test scores from the program. He was looking for votes.

Mayor Kunsmiller was an interesting politician. Controversial, ever in the news, he was the stereotype of the media politician. Always grandstanding, always running for office, always available for comment. How well he managed the city was a matter of disagreement, assuming the city was manageable. Now, running for another term, his political skill was demonstrated by the fact he was running on both the Democratic and Republican tickets. Made things simpler for the voters that way.

Reeder caught a taxi to the Mayor's office. He was expected at ten. Velma Williams rose from her chair to greet him. She was tall, well built, her shapely thighs displayed in a short skirt well above her knees. Her black hair was cut short in a severe bob. A sexy woman. She might have stepped off the set of *Caberet*. She looked to be in her mid-30s, a little old to be wearing such a short skirt. Reeder wondered why. She certainly had the legs for it.

"We are so glad to have you working with us," she said. "We have heard good things about you from several people."

At forty-five Reeder had been bouncing around the evaluation field for nearly twenty years, and he had heard all the talk. But it was still difficult for him to pick out the ceremonial bullshit from sincere compliments. Or was it because he was sucked in by such comments, his experience notwithstanding? A personality weakness.

"Good to be here. Sounds like a fascinating project."

He had his own ceremonial line of bullshit for clients. No matter how dull or routine the program, he told them it was fascinating. He noted there was no one else in the office. Just the two of them. Maybe she wanted to get some things straight before bringing any one else in.

"Did you look at the material we sent you?"

"Yes, I looked it over. The monitoring project is loosely defined. But that's ok. I don't mind working in ambiguous situations. I gather I am supposed to keep tabs on the evaluation done by the school district and say whether it's adequate. Not do the study or take part in it."

"Yes, that's right. You can give advice too, if you want. We don't have the expertise in this office to tell whether the evaluation is ok. Nor do we have the credibility to make our opinion stick even if we did. To be perfectly frank, some of us opposed the Second Chance program. We thought it would cost too much and wouldn't work. But the Mayor decided to go ahead with it."

"Yes, I saw him on television this morning, saying he had raised the test scores in New York City. Standing in front of an elementary school."

"He's a good politician. A brilliant politician. He doesn't always get the policy angle right though. He has an instinct as to what will play well with the public. Sometimes what he wants works, sometimes it doesn't. Our job in this office is to try to sort out the two. And head off trouble."

"I guess he's no different from any politician in that regard."

"Not really. He's just better at the politicking than most. Comes natural."

"If it should turn out the program doesn't work, that the evaluation says the program is not working. What then?"

"We'll worry about that when and if it happens. I suspect the Mayor will just go on to something else. At least, that's what he has done in the past."

"Won't he be embarrassed by the failure?"

"Not if we handle it right. One thing we expect is that your reports to us will be confidential. Sent to us and the Chancellor's office alone. No one else."

So this was what she wanted when she met with him one on one. Secrecy. Confidential monitoring reports not released to the public. That way they could control the PR damage. Or try to.

"Usually, evaluations are public. At least in this country. In Britain it's different. They have a tradition of public secrecy. You could be subject to the Official Secrets Act in Britain if you told someone how many chairs were in a room in a government building, theoretically at least. We have a tradition of open government in the U.S., the CIA and FBI notwithstanding."

He was playing his hand cautiously, telling her what normal procedures were. He didn't like secret evaluations. They had problems. Especially when clients didn't like the findings. They could bury the study without anyone knowing anything. And clients always overestimated the good things the evaluation would turn up. When the evaluation churned out negative findings, clients reacted negatively. Human nature.

Suppressing the evaluation was typical. So what you did was get them to agree in advance to how the report would be made public. And to whom. They usually agreed since they expected positive findings, even praise, from the evaluation. Reeder had never agreed to do a confidential study before.

"Of course," she was saying, "the evaluation studies done by the district will be made public. It is only your monitoring reports that will be confidential. Your reports will go only to our office and the Chancellor's office." She had repeated it.

Reeder thought for a moment. He hadn't expected this, even after the meeting last night with the Chancellor's henchmen when they tried to impress on him who was paying. With the Mayor's office he was dealing with a level of political sophistication far above that of his typical clients. He thought about the possibilities.

He could insist his reports be made public. He was sure she would say no. He guessed that confidentiality was part of the understanding between the Mayor and the Chancellor. They had decided that already. The Chancellor's office didn't want the monitoring to begin with. They sure as hell didn't want the monitoring reports made public saying that their evaluation was a bunch of crap, if it came to that.

For her part she could use the confidential reports to bargain with the Chancellor if she needed to. And she didn't need the reports public for that. In fact, better not. She could negotiate the phase out of the program quietly behind the scenes, if necessary. Also, public disclosure of his reports would focus attention on the monitoring, which would give Reeder bargaining power and a say in the disposition of the program. He would be a public authority. The Mayor's office didn't want that either. Too much out of their control.

The downside for him was that he could do the monitoring and have his work buried if it was politically expedient. All the work for nothing. And the public interest betrayed. He could give up the whole enterprise right now. But he knew they could find someone else to do it, someone more compliant.

On the other hand, he was dealing with a massive bureaucracy containing thousands of disaffected employees, conflicts of interest, and different points of view buried within it. What were the chances they could keep the reports secret even if they tried? Not much, he figured.

He also knew something else. The parent union was aware he was coming to New York even before he had been notified. There was a leak somewhere already. He knew something she didn't. Or did he?

"Ok," Reeder said. "I will do it confidentially. I'll send one copy of my report to the Mayor's office and one copy to the Chancellor's office. No other copies. What happens to the reports after that is your responsibility. My experience is that confidential reports don't stay confidential in large organizations."

He had given her his best guess as to what was likely to happen, as he had given the Chancellor's men advice about the difficulty of increasing test scores. Informing them met his sense of his ethical obligation when he didn't agree with clients. He explained things to them. Whether they took his advice was up to them.

"That's our worry. We'll expect your first monitoring report after you have a chance to look at what the district evaluators have done so far. There are several documents."

"Ok. Give me a week to sort things out and catch up. The evaluation office is sending me the materials."

"Are you heading straight back right away or are you staying in town tonight?" she asked.

A curious question. An expression of interest? Professional courtesy? His imagination? He didn't know.

"I have a 5 o'clock plane back this afternoon," Reeder said, making a mental note. She rose to shake his hand goodbye.

CHAPTER FIVE

Dozens of airplanes were lined up on the LaGuardia runway waiting to take off. It was an hour before his plane lifted into the air, and the 2-hour flight back was bumpy, with the flight attendants struggling on their feet to deliver the service. He found his car in the parking lot and drove home.

From the outside his house was impressive. A two-story art deco building with curved lines, surfaced with stucco, an unusual style for the town. Inside it was masculine. It was clear that no woman lived there. The place was sparsely furnished to the point of being bare. Not a single plant. Books lined the walls and lay stacked on tables and chairs. Paintings sat on the floor against the wall.

After his wife left, Reeder had meant to hang the paintings but never got around to it. That was eleven years ago. When a friend said she thought it was a trendy way of displaying artwork, Reeder liked the idea and left the paintings where they sat. Maybe he would hang them some day, for variety.

He took off his suit and hung it in the closet. His suits were an extravagance, hand-tailored. When he did business in Washington, the suits were an advantage. Even more so in Europe, where people immediately eyed the cut and material. They treated you differently, depending on how well you were dressed. An unfortunate fact of life, but a fact. He never wore suits on campus.

Reeder checked his voice mail. A call from a graduate student wanting to know if he could read her dissertation proposal in the next two days. Students spent years working on their proposals and expected you to respond in a few days. He could let the call go until tomorrow.

He poured himself a glass of red wine from an open bottle sitting on the counter and flipped on the television to catch the news. Not much happening. Reporters ritually following the president around as if flying off the White House lawn in a helicopter was an event of significance. The simple physical movement of the president from one place to another was treated with the same public regard as the Sun King's toilet, Reeder thought. And it was just as meaningful. He flipped through the channels looking for financial news, in no mood for presidential bombast.

Reeder's taste in food defied simplicity. For the past year, he had been living on pasta and canned tuna. He didn't tire of them. Before that he had lived on frozen dinners, and before that on pizza. He wondered what that said about him. He threw a package of angel hair pasta into a pan of water and looked for a bottle of olive oil. He balanced his monotonous diet by eating out several times a week. Tonight he decided to combine his two favorite dishes by dumping a can of tuna into the pasta and dousing the mixture liberally with olive oil. Haut cuisine.

When he was married, he had a more varied diet. Life without his wife was simpler in many ways, though not better. He could eat what he wanted, when he wanted, and drink what he wanted. Nonetheless, he had not wanted her to leave. She thought he was far too critical. He set standards no woman could meet. She had gone to Chicago and was happy there, from what he could tell, taking up with a man who was more supportive. Since then his problem was not with getting along with women but getting along with too many. Or maybe that was the same thing. Lack of commitment.

He remembered Andrew Neil's assertion that men were naturally polygamous while women were monogamous. A self-serving contention, no doubt. Still, Reeder wondered whether it was true. He wasn't sure. If it were true, it had helped neither Neil nor himself since they had both ended up alone. Or was that how they wanted it? He wasn't sure about that either. Neither made moves to change.

Reeder finished off the pasta and leaned back in his chair with the remains of the wine to think about the New York project. It was complex, and he didn't know where he was. It wasn't unusual to be baffled early in a project, to feel you didn't know where you were or even whether you could bring the thing off. This one was so high profile and the contending forces so powerful he worried how to manage it. Maybe he would give Neil a call tomorrow to see what he thought.

He stripped off and climbed naked between the cool sheets. You could feel a chill in the air. Who knew what winter would bring? This was a land of extremes.

CHAPTER SIX

When he arrived at his office next morning, he became irritated. He had forgotten there was a faculty meeting at 10 o'clock. Just what he needed, another worthless faculty meeting when he had projects and papers to work on. By the time he got through his mail it was time for the meeting. He met Boyer in the hallway.

"Christ, what's on the agenda today?"

"Curriculum requirements," Boyer said. "Same old stuff."

"I thought we settled that two months ago."

"Yes, but some of the faculty think their courses are being slighted with the new requirements."

Faculty meetings were events you had rather not be at, in Reeder's view. No matter how much time there was to discuss an issue, faculty members talked long enough to fill the time available. Having words as the focus of their lives led to vocational disabilities. Nowhere was this better displayed than in faculty meetings.

The dean began the meeting by reading bulletins from the university administration. Telling people news they could read for themselves proved irresistible to administrators for some reason. The faculty sat patiently, listening to the dean drone on. Finally to the main item of business.

"Some faculty have raised questions about the curriculum requirements for the master's degree we agreed to earlier. I thought we would open the discussion to hear any objections."

One of the prerogatives of faculty life was that anyone could say anything about anything, even if they knew nothing about it. There had even been suggestions that faculty members should not criticize what other faculty said because that might stifle free expression. Reeder imagined what endless talk without criticism might be like. An infinite expansion of hot air. He shuddered.

"I don't think the students are exposed to enough research methodology," Lisa Brinkley said. She taught the beginning research course, and the students were reluctant to take the course because of her poor teaching. Enrollments were dropping.

"Not enough background in sociology of the field either," Antonio Valdez said.

He taught the sociology courses.

Self-interest was disguised as concern for students so that requirements increased in proportion to the needs of the faculty rather than those of the students. As transparent as this ploy was, no faculty member dared challenged it as self-interest. The rules of discourse were that you had to respond in terms of presumed student needs, not in terms of real faculty motivations. Of course, private conversations were another matter. In private faculty members lambasted each other's motives, character, and abilities.

"Yes, but if we require these courses in addition to those we have now, it will take another semester for students to complete the degree," Boyer said. He had engineered the last compromise on course requirements and was reluctant to let that work slip away. The faculty was staring at months of effort if they reopened the requirements.

"I don't see why we can't just let students take what courses they want," the new woman who taught elementary education said.

Reeder couldn't remember her name. You could tell from looking at the way she was dressed that she was into letting spirits roam free. Reeder slid down in his hard chair. This was going to be a long session, not that any were short.

The last remark brought the dean back into the discussion. "We can't just let them take what they want. There are state requirements that have to be met."

"We have to explain to the state that students have needs for freedom and autonomy that have to be met too," the free spirit woman said. "They have a behaviorist philosophy of human nature that is all wrong. It's our responsibility to enlighten them so they can see what damage requirements can do."

The image of going to the state capital and enlightening the legislators about the futility of state mandates flashed through Reeder's mind. He looked across the room at Barrett, the statistics man, who was staring at the floor while pounding himself in his forehead with his fist, as if this was more than he could take.

Reeder attempted a diversion. "Why don't we try the current requirements for a year and see how they work. We can change them if it appears the students are not prepared properly."

Reeder knew there was no way they could tell a year from now, or any year for that matter, whether the students were prepared. The faculty made up the tests the students had to pass, which was the only method used to determine what students knew. It was a closed circle. But such a move would postpone the issue for a year. And Reeder knew it was difficult for them to argue against experimenting and evaluating. It was part of their professional ideology.

Several people concurred, inspired by a way out. The compromise was set. Yet discussion dragged on for an hour. Edison fell asleep during the talk, nodding off from time to time, then waking up abruptly only to doze off again. He was well into his 70s. Every year he filed an age discrimination complaint with the university over his pay increase, which he considered inadequate. No doubt he would hire a lawyer eventually, if he didn't fall asleep in a faculty meeting and not wake up before that happened.

Reeder was resigned. Some things in life you had to bear, and faculty meetings were one of these. The idea of faculty self-governance sounded ideally democratic. It worked out differently in actuality. On the other hand, letting university administrators make decisions was hardly a desirable alternative. They brought their own disabilities to the table.

Reeder thought about the new administration building. There was no men's toilet for two floors up or down. When the building was planned, the top administrators did not want the dean of continuing education to move to the new building with the others. But no one had the temerity to face him to tell him he wasn't moving. He was staying in the old building. When the new building was nearing completion, the dean found out and raised hell. As a result, the planned toilets were converted into office space for him, at extra cost. No toilets for two floors. At least the building provided opportunity for exercise.

The faculty meeting was winding down because faculty had classes to teach. As Reeder anticipated, the dean appointed a committee to revisit the requirement issue next year and determine whether student needs were being met. Unfortunately, as the evaluation expert and the one who suggested the idea, Reeder was put on the committee. The dean ended the meeting by saying what an excellent discussion of the issues this had been and that the faculty had arrived at the most judicious decision.

Reeder hurried back to his office to find two phone messages waiting. First, though, he wanted to call Andrew Neil to see if it was all right to drop by after work to talk about the New York project.

CHAPTER SEVEN

Reeder arrived at Neil's house at five-thirty. Neil insisted on living in a small house in a working class neighborhood, his effort to renounce the pretensions of the professional middle-class, in his view. Neil opened the door holding a large glass of whiskey in one hand and a cigarette in the other. He had started drinking already. The house was filled with a haze of smoke.

"Hah!" he said, obviously delighted to see Reeder. "How about a little nip of whiskey before dinner? I like to drink while I cook."

"Ok, but not too much. I have to drive," Reeder said. He was a wine drinker but when he was with Neil he drank whiskey. Whiskey was an important part of Neil's life. The consequences had been some of the worst hangovers of Reeder's experience, which was saying something.

"How are things on campus?"

Neil had been retired for five years and still retained an office on campus. Though he appeared sporadically, he knew more than Reeder about what was going on. He wanted to hear what Reeder would say. Even though Neil had been in the United States for thirty years, he had never lost his strong Scottish accent. In fact, it seemed stronger than ever. Sometimes you had to listen carefully through the thick burr to understand what he was saying.

"Same old crap. And having a weak dean doesn't help."

"No other kind, is there?"

Although Neil had been director of the evaluation center for years, he never lost his virulent antiauthoritarianism. It had gotten him into trouble. And had caused even more trouble for university administrators. One reason the center had prospered under Neil was that the administrators wanted no part of him. He was insufficiently respectful, to say the least. As a result the center had more space and special privileges than any other unit. Counterintuitive really.

Reeder took the glass of whiskey, filled far higher than he had asked for, and sank into the couch. Most of Neil's furnishings had been purchased second-hand at flea markets and garage sales. Neil loved to look for bargains. His Scottish ancestry. The house was jammed with an assortment of items gathered with no regard for style, though he favored art nouveau, especially ripe nudes. Even his dishes were bought in second-hand markets.

"How do you like that whiskey?"

"Ok, but it tastes a little chemical to me," Reeder said, making a face.

"Yes, that's an island malt. They are like that." This was an authoritative pronouncement. Nothing more to be said.

"So you've been to New York," Neil said. "New project?"

"Yes. A new project."

Since Neil had hired him at the center, when Reeder had a difficult project, he talked to Neil about it. As a founder of the evaluation field, Neil had long experience with complex projects. He had spent his career building up the center. And though he never published much, no one was better at sorting out the politics of the craft. Neil's thinking was so devious he readily detected the suspicious motivations of others.

Neil finished his whiskey and stepped into the small kitchen to rinse his glass before refilling it. Reeder glanced at the paintings on the walls, mostly originals by amateurs, not bad for the most part. He focused on a new one showing a nude woman being pursued by a horny goat in a Mediterranean landscape. Yes, that seems about right, Reeder thought. Neil's problems with women surpassed his own. Neil's wife had run off years ago. The action was hardly unprovoked.

The cigarette smoke was making Reeder's eyes water. He rose to open a window to let in fresh air. At that moment Neil returned to the room.

"Don't open the window!" he said. "You'll let the smoke out!" Neil closed it before Reeder could say a thing.

"The smoke is bothering my eyes," Reeder said.

"Nonsense. Smoke's good for you. Don't tell me you've become one of these fascists opposed to smoking. What's the matter with you? Don't you believe in civil rights?"

Reeder declined to take up the challenge. And hopeless. Neil chain-smoked one cigarette after the other. It was difficult for him to go ten minutes without one. Which made travel increasingly difficult. He arranged erratic overseas flights on the basis of which airlines allowed smoking. When you were with him, you were tempted to smoke too, for self-protection. In spite of whiskey, cigarettes, and lack of exercise, he looked younger than his age, which he kept secret.

Reeder knew how old Neil was but few did. A woman who worked with Neil claimed she knew his age because she had peeked at an official document he was filling out. The age Neil put on the document was ten years younger than his real age, Reeder knew. Reeder figured that Neil pretended to hide the age he wrote on the document but allowed the woman to see it so she would think that was his actual age. A devious mind. And a very clever one.

By this time the whiskey was seeping into Reeder's brain. It never failed. He would have to eat something before he drove home. This was dangerous. Neil poured him another glass and another for himself. Reeder didn't protest.

"Why don't you stay and have dinner with me? Unless you have other plans. I have a seafood casserole on the stove left over from two nights ago. Plenty of it left too."

"You have seafood casserole sitting out for two nights ago? You can't eat that. It'll make you sick!"

"Nonsense. People exaggerate these things. I don't get sick from food poisoning that often. Maybe once or twice a month. Food poisoning isn't that bad."

"No left over seafood casserole."

Reeder was worried that he might drink too much whiskey and end up eating the casserole anyhow. He had done worse things when drinking with Neil.

"Ok, ok, if you stay I'll fix my macaroni and cheese special with bacon over the top. One of your favorites."

This was the way sessions with Neil went. Lots of whisky. Lots of talk. Sometimes brilliant talk. Neil was a great talker. Unfortunately, the next morning it was difficult to remember what was said the night before.

CHAPTER EIGHT

By the time the macaroni and cheese were ready, they had downed another whiskey, though Reeder slowed down, knowing he had to work next day and that drinking with Neil was a disaster. He wanted Neil's insights about the New York project. And he wanted to remember them. Reeder brought the topic around to the reason for his visit.

"Let me ask your advice about the New York project."

He knew that once primed, there was no stopping Neil. Reeder outlined what he knew so far, taking care to provide details of the politics. Neil listened intently, dragging on a cigarette from time to time, squinting, and sipping whiskey from his heavy whiskey glass.

"Reminds me of a project in the South," Neil said. "An evaluation of the state police. One of my worst projects ever."

Neil had developed expertise in evaluating police training, an unlikely specialty given his antiauthoritarian attitude. That made it more challenging, from his point of view. This state was notorious for corruption.

"I didn't know what I was getting into. No idea. When I arrived in the state, nineteen of the top officials were in jail, and the twentieth should have been. But he was the governor and had managed to escape prosecution."

"Why did they ask you in? Or did they? Sounds to me as if that's hardly a situation for an evaluator to be in."

"They were deadlocked. The reformers, the police union, and the government. They needed to break their deadlock. They heard about my other police evaluations. Like a fool I went in not knowing what I was getting into."

"What happened?"

"Well, I went by myself first of all, thinking I could pick up help. Big mistake. I should have brought my own team, people I could count on.

And when I arrived, the police lodged me directly across the street from police headquarters where they could keep an eye on me. They knew everyone who came to talk to me. I wouldn't be surprised if the place was bugged."

"Couldn't you find anyone to help you?" Reeder said, recalling his experiences.

"Trouble was I ran afoul of the reformers. I didn't have much time to do the project so when I met them I asked them straight out, 'What's in this for you?' Bad question to begin with."

"Shit! I'll bet that went down well!"

At times Neil could ask brilliant questions. He might listen to a public official spew out the party line in an interview for an hour and ask him, "What do you worry about as a person when you lie awake at night?" As often as not, the official would step out of the prescribed role and reveal candid assessments of the program. Neil knew that people played roles and that they could tell the difference between their role behavior and their personal beliefs.

At other times, with his unconventional thinking, Neil asked questions that backfired and alienated the people he was interviewing. Asking the reformers what was in it for them was a misfire. It didn't fit the reformers' view of themselves. They would be insulted.

"Why in the hell did you ask that?"

"Lack of time. I was in a hurry, working by myself, no backup. I needed to get a report out pronto. So I tried to take a shortcut. Of course, it didn't work."

"What did they do? Oppose you?"

"Well, yes, and I was forced to attack their position anyhow. They wanted to appoint a civilian head of the police. I opposed that plan once I understood the situation. The police would simply have resisted the reforms, and nothing would have happened to change the corruption in the force, which was deep-seated. I wanted the police to reform themselves from the inside. The only way reform ever works."

"How do you mean, through training and taking responsibility themselves?"

Neil's belief about bureaucracies was that they could oppose reforms effectively if they wanted, even when they appeared to be cooperating. Outsiders could not penetrate the operations of these organizations enough to shape daily behavior. And daily behavior was what mattered. Reforms had to be internalized by those in the organization to have any chance of success. That was a tall order and required a long-term perspective. Politicians couldn't tolerate long-term solutions to problems. They needed quick fixes.

By this time they had finished eating and Neil was pouring water into his instant coffee, which he thrived on when he wasn't drinking whiskey.

"Want some coffee?"

Reeder looked at the instant coffee and felt his stomach churn. He knew he should drink something to sober up but raw instant coffee was not that appealing.

"How about some tea?"

Neil dropped a tea bag into a cup and poured the boiling water over it. Reeder dipped the bag into the hot water a few moments and removed the tea bag with his spoon, wrapping the string around the spoon. He put it on his plate.

"What are you doing?" Neil said, exhaling a lungful of smoke.

"You'll stain my spoons!"

Reeder looked at the worn spoon, no doubt bought in a garage sale like Neil's other tableware. The outer layer had worn through.

"You are getting to be a fussy old lady in your old age."

Neil had lived by himself long enough that he was developing quirky habits. Reeder wondered about himself too.

"I don't want you ruining my spoons."

"What else happened in the project?"

"Well, there were many players with conflicting interests, all wanting something different. That's like your New York project," Neil said, picking bits of pasta from his teeth and lighting a cigarette.

"Yes, you can say that again. How did you handle that?"

"Badly. When I wrote my report, I included something for everyone. I directed portions of the report to different groups. Some to the reformers, some to the police, some to the people at the university who would do the police training, some to the public."

"Wouldn't that be a little incoherent?" Reeder imagined what such a report would look like. He could see different pieces not fitting together.

"It was worse than that. It was a disaster. The chief of police lampooned the report before the state legislature. He read passages of it aloud, passages I intended for the people at the university. Of course, those theoretical statements sounded pompous when read to the public. You know how pretentious sociology sounds."

"Christ, that was a disaster! How did you recover from that?"

"I didn't. The nastiest thing was the chief went on television and said he never liked me from the beginning. Worst of all, he called me English!" Neil referred to his Scottish background. For a man who dragged his pregnant wife across the border so his child would be born in Scotland, being called English was a serious affront.

"I thought the report would be like a Christmas tree, something for everybody dangling from it, but it backfired. The whole thing backfired.

When a reporter asked me on television what I thought about the chief of police saying he never like me, all I could say was, 'I liked him. I guess he must be a better judge of character than I am.' Clever, I thought. A good parting shot. But I resigned a few days later. There was nothing I could do. I was finished."

"It does sound like a disaster. And not unlike the New York situation with all the contending parties."

"If I were doing that one—which I might not take on, by the way—I would have a team of people to help me, my own people. People I could count on. And I would not write a report like I did. Also, I would give myself plenty of time. Not a few weeks. You need time to sort things out in such complicated politics."

Neil was filling the air with smoke again. And heading for the liquor shelf in his living room. The shelf held a wide assortment of malt whiskies, some quite expensive. Whiskey was one thing he would spend money on.

"How about a little nip before you head home?"

"No, have to drive home."

Neil's driving record provided incentives to lay off the whiskey.

CHAPTER NINE

Reeder had already thought about establishing a team of people he could rely on. Neil confirmed that idea. For one thing a lot hinged on the analysis of the test scores. In such a contentious atmosphere any interpretation of test results was likely to be challenged. He needed expertise that would be unchallengeable, or if not, at least likely to carry the day when the crunch came.

Fortunately, the center had one of the leading test expert in the country, Barry Winslow. The problem was that Winslow was so busy advising government agencies he might not have time. Although others had the expertise to do the job, they lacked the reputation, critical in a high profile project. Reeder would have to persuade Winslow.

The curriculum focus of the New York program was reading and math. Reeder knew that the teaching of reading was politicized. Phonics, sight, whole instruction. Scholars had conflicting ideas and ripped their rivals apart in constant sniping. Few could be as vicious as early childhood experts, except possibly religious scholars. He could use help to guide him through the minefield. Walter Rusk was a good choice. Rusk was energetic and well read. Solid.

That would leave the team with no women or minorities, always a consideration. No doubt such a deficiency would be noted and criticized. It would diminish the credibility of the team. It was difficult to take on an enterprise without minority and female representation. Eighty percent of the students in the Second Chance program were minorities. It would be good to have some perspective on that.

Reeder didn't resent the intrusion of minority and gender politics. He had served on enough committees to know that committee members treated minority and gender matters differently if there were representatives of those groups present. The presence of a woman or a minority made committee members aware of issues in a way they were not if there were none there. Committee work turned out differently, even if the women or minorities didn't say a word.

On the other hand, Reeder also knew that women and minorities could be pains in the ass if they saw everything from one perspective only, so that everything reduced to one issue. One issue in the whole world. There were plenty of people around like that.

Reeder figured he should add Maria Garcia to the team. She was militant enough that she would speak her mind and also willing to look at the larger framework. Four was enough for the team. If he added more people it would be difficult to manage. Getting even four people together was tough.

Reeder waited a week until the New York materials arrived. These included the plan for the evaluation and the studies the district had conducted so far. He sent copies to his colleagues and scheduled a meeting.

Everyone showed up for the meeting in the small conference room, and Reeder began by presenting his assessment of the evaluation plan. The plan needed balance to the complete reliance on tests, in his view. Winslow went next.

"It seems to me there is a serious problem with the way they have analyzed their summer programs," he said.

"How do you mean?" Rusk asked.

"They give the reading tests in April, and if the students don't achieve a high enough score, they must go to summer school for eight weeks."

"Right, and the summer curriculum is tuned to the test itself," Rusk said, ready to make another point.

"Don't know about that. But at the end of summer they give the same test to the students again. If they pass, the students go on to next grade. If they fail, they must repeat the grade they were in."

"What's wrong with that?"

"They haven't taken into account the regression to the mean."

The others were puzzled. Winslow explained.

"It's complicated, an artifact of testing. Suppose you give a test to a group of students. Some students will be sick the day they take the test and won't do well. Other students will skip a page in the test booklet accidentally and miss the test items on that page. Still others will get the fill-in boxes mixed up."

"Yes, everyone knows that," Rusk said. "But when you give the test again, those students will do ok. The sick student will be healthy, the one who skipped the page won't do it again, and so on. Their scores will be what they should have been without the problems. And some others will make the same errors. It will be balanced. The averages of the two groups will be the same."

Regression to the Mean   31

"Ah, yes. But suppose that after you give the test the first time, you *separate out* the lowest performing students, including those who made those accidental errors. Let's say you put them, *and only them,* in summer school. Then, when you give the test the second time, you give the test *only* to those low scorers who went to summer school. Their scores will improve—compared to their first scores—because they won't make the same errors again, as you say. The scores will improve because they weren't sick or confused this time around."

"So what?" Rusk said. "I don't get it. What's the point?"

"The point is that the school district is giving the test twice and taking the difference between the first test and the second test as gains resulting from being in summer school. In fact, the gain may be from what we are talking about. Mistakes made the first time but not the second time from other causes. Not gains from knowing more answers."

"You mean the student test scores might improve because of this artificial effect and not from instruction?" Garcia said.

"I mean they could give the same test twice and the scores would show improvement even if there had been no instruction at all. Even if the students didn't learn a thing. It's an artifact of testing. Other things being equal, of course."

Winslow was cautious in his interpretations and slow to draw radical conclusions. Reeder was thinking this issue could be serious.

"Wait a minute," Reeder said. "This is all very theoretical. We don't know if this has happened. Only that it *might* have happened. How can we tell for sure? We can't go around accusing the school district of misinterpreting their own data without evidence."

"Oh, it happened," Winslow said. "It's just a matter of statistics in a sense. The question is how big a difference does it make? How big an effect is it in this particular case? How far off are they?"

"Well, how far off are they?" Reeder repeated. "Is there a way of telling that?"

"Yes, you can estimate the size of the regression effect if you know other characteristics of the test. This is one of the most common tests around, the Cosmopolitan Reading test. There is a formula for estimating the regression effect."

"Well, could you estimate this if you had their test data?"

"I don't need their data. I have enough information from the evaluation studies they sent us."

The others were astounded.

"How big an effect, is it then?" Reeder knew Winslow was a stickler for precision. Although Reeder was alarmed at Winslow's analysis of the New York data, he figured the effect would be small, something he would have to mention to be technically accurate, the price of bringing Winslow on board. It would be of no practical significance and could be dealt with in a footnote.

"I estimate the effect to be roughly equivalent to what they claim their test gains are," Winslow said.

The other three were stunned. No one said anything. Winslow had scrambled their thoughts.

After a few seconds, Reeder said, "You mean they have no test gains from their summer program? They just think they do?"

"I don't think so, at least if my analysis is correct."

"Can you check your analysis to be sure you have it right?"

"Yes, I can. But I'm pretty sure."

"The Mayor of New York is standing in front of an elementary school saying he raised the test scores in the city as his major campaign accomplishment and, in fact, there are no gains?" Reeder repeated the information for himself as much as for anyone else.

"Looks like it."

They turned to other issues. Rusk discussed the curriculum, and Garcia noted how the program might affect minorities. Reeder listened but kept thinking about Winslow's analysis. If there were no test gains, someone was going to be in deep shit. And Reeder had a sinking feeling who that might be.

CHAPTER TEN

The next Wednesday Reeder flew to Washington for an advisory council meeting at the National Science Foundation. Washington was one of the few places you could reach from the cornfields without changing planes. The connection reflected the importance of the federal government to the university's research funding. University personnel regularly made the trip, hauling paper in and money out. Reeder glanced around the plane to see familiar faces. Though he didn't know all their names, he knew their departments.

The flight took two hours, landing in a drizzle at Dulles Airport. The long taxi ride into the city gave him time to change gears in his thinking. This was a trip he made many times a year when he did business with federal agencies. As the taxi passed the CIA turn-off, Reeder noted that someone had taken down the Central Intelligence Agency road sign. The CIA must have been the only spy organization in the world with two-foot high letters announcing its location. Americans felt ambivalent about secret government.

The traffic slowed abruptly as two highways converged. The taxi crept along the Potomac River until suddenly the monuments and buildings on the government mall became visible. As they crossed the Key Bridge, Reeder looked at the lights shining on the Washington Monument and the Lincoln Memorial, elegant in their classic forms.

"You guys really know how to build a capital," a French woman had said as he showed her around the government mall. A high compliment from someone from Paris. He wondered what had happened to her. He had lost touch. She had been provocative as they stood on the steps of the Capital.

"Look at the Washington Monument rising like a giant erection. Look at these columns all over the place. If anybody ever had any doubt what this country is about, all they have to do is come to Washington to see the architecture. Assertion and power! The place is so phallic it's obscene!"

It was too Freudian for him. But she had a point. Nations expressed their ambitions in architecture. Since then he puzzled over whatever capital city he was in, wondering what the buildings signified. In the hotel room the woman found a little paper facsimile of the Washington Monument and took it home with her as a remembrance of Washington and of him. She saw the two fitting together.

As the taxi crawled through the thick evening traffic, Reeder watched hundreds of workers leaving their offices after 7 PM, going home late. Contrary to stereotypes, federal workers put in long hours. The effectiveness of the programs they administered was more questionable.

In the center of the city, he noticed dozens of people living on the streets. Some were trying to get under doorways and arcades to protect themselves from the rain. Others claimed the grills in the middle of the boulevards, ignoring the rain. Hot air issued from the grills and offered relief from the damp cold. Some had set up house with old couches and chairs dragged over the grills, as if they were sitting in their living rooms. As often as he saw the homeless, he was shocked. What kind of country did he live in?

The taxi glided past the White House, glistening under lights in its unreal white coating. As the taxi stopped at a small hotel a few blocks away, Reeder noted the high cost of the trip. No one wanted to use public transport when they came to Washington at night. It was too dangerous. Or people thought it was too dangerous. One colleague had been pursued by a carload of youths as he strolled down the street. Everyone had stories. Perhaps eventually visitors would be picked up in armored taxis at the airport and dropped off underground at their hotels.

He paid the driver, asked for a receipt, and walked into the hotel. There was a package waiting for him at the desk, reading material for the meeting tomorrow. Officials in Washington were rarely able to get materials to participants in advance. Either events changed so rapidly that only today mattered or officials lost track of time. Reeder went to his small room, took a shower, put on a suit, and left the hotel.

CHAPTER ELEVEN

He had arranged to meet Elizabeth at a restaurant near Capital Hill, a French place a favorite of politicians, not as expensive as many in the city. It was one of her favorites. They dined there often in the old days. As usual she was running late. He had a glass of wine while he waited.

When she came in, he felt the old feelings surge through him as he saw her. She was a little heavier now, more matronly. That's what age and having a kid had done. But she was still very attractive, he thought. And still dressed in expensive clothes. She scanned the bar area, knowing where he would be. Her face glowed when she saw him.

"How are you?" she said, kissing him on the mouth. "You look good. Still keeping fit, I see."

"You too. You haven't changed a bit." That wasn't quite true, but close enough, he figured. He held his arms around her for a moment. He had forgotten how small her body was. She was more delicate than him in every way.

They found a table near the back of the restaurant and sat down to catch up with one another. He noticed she still wore beige colors that went with her light brown hair. She was excited to see him.

"How is your son?" he said, knowing this would be foremost on her mind.

"Fantastic! John is doing so well in school he is unbelievable. The teachers are really impressed with him. They think he is absolutely exceptional. He won an essay contest for the entire school. His teacher said it was worthy of a much older student." She gushed when she talked about her son. Reeder remembered Yeats's line about whether mothers would think their investment in their sons worthwhile if they could see their boys when they were elderly. He resisted the temptation to cite it. Elizabeth would think the investment worthwhile, in any case.

Her son's academic progress was the most important thing in her life. That and her career. She was a lawyer in a high-powered Washington law firm. Highly successful. The effort she did not expend on her son she put into her work. Her husband was secondary. That had been true when she and Reeder had been seeing each other before her son was born. It was still true, except that now her son was the emotional focus that Reeder had been.

"What about Larry?"

"He is the same. Getting along in this job in accounting. For however long it lasts." Her tone was flat as she talked about her husband. She married someone she expected to have a brilliant career. That had not panned out. He jumped from one job to another without being particularly successful. No use talking about it. They had discussed her disappointment in the old days.

It had been more than seven years since they quit seeing each other. After his marriage fractured, Reeder had been desolate, isolated. Elizabeth was the first woman he had opened up to. The first one he trusted enough to allow himself to be vulnerable with. A breakthrough into a zone of intimacy he had not experienced before.

"I have given up on Larry ever amounting to anything. So we are about the same as usual. It's ok, really. I just have to lower my expectations. Which I did long ago." She made the best of what she had and didn't bitch about it. He wished he had that quality.

Much of her appeal was that she said whatever came into her mind. No matter if it was socially incorrect. She said what she felt. There was a remarkable emotional transparency about her. Perhaps that enabled him to trust her. He knew what she was thinking because she said it.

"How about you? Anybody new?"

He knew what she meant. Right to the point. Never mind his kids or his work. She wanted to know about his love life. Said exactly what was on her mind.

"No, no one new. At least no one serious."

She looked relieved. Still jealous after all these years, he noted. It was strange how they were able to reestablish conversation on an intimate level so soon, even when they hadn't seen each other for a year. They lapsed back into warm affection, seeking each other out. He knew she was truly concerned about what was happening to him. He knew she wanted him to be happy.

"Are you happy?" she said.

"I'm ok." Actually, he wasn't sure. But if he said he didn't know he would have to explain. He didn't think he could. He knew her question was more than a simple inquiry. It had a history.

Years ago, she wanted him to live with her. He agonized about it and decided against it. After his failed marriage, he didn't want to make another commitment. Maybe there were other reasons he didn't recognize. Eventually, she decided her time was running out. She wanted children. Child rearing ended the relationship. Ironically, after she recommitted herself to her marriage, he was more inclined. By then she had her son.

The wine arrived and he lifted his glass to her.

"To us."

"To us," she said, smiling, touching her glass to his, and squeezing his hand with her free hand. She looked into his eyes.

"You still have the most complex, beautiful eyes I have ever seen in a man."

"You are beautiful too. A beautiful woman." She glowed at the compliment. No fending it off with false modesty. She was a beautiful woman, he thought. Even at her age.

"And you are still my real man," she said.

In the old days she called him her real man, to distinguish him from others she had known. Something to do with integrity, reliability, courage. He wasn't sure of the criteria but he knew what she meant.

The arrival of appetizers interrupted their conversation. She asked about his work, and he told her about the New York project. She listened intently. She knew New York well and made good suggestions. He used to test new ideas out on her. Not only did it enhance their intimacy, it improved his work.

As they talked, she ate only part of her appetizer, half her fish course. She ate what filled her and let the rest go. This amazed him. It reflected their different backgrounds. When he was young, he knew what it was to be hungry. She grew up in a wealthy family, and the idea there might not be enough food never occurred to her. It would still never occur to her. She was as refined as he was rough.

She found his rough background appealing. She was fascinated with stories about his childhood, marveled at what different worlds they grew up in. Different social classes, different cultures, different body types.

"What am I doing with a football player?" she said after an athletic sexual encounter.

When he first saw her in a white suit standing on a staircase in Washington, he thought her angelic. Trim, expensively dressed, cosmopolitan, outside his realm, beyond his reach. Only when she displayed undeniable interest in him did he consider her a possibility. And it caught him by surprise.

After a few months acquaintance, they went to a bookstore and stopped in a café for coffee. They chatted about books for a few moments. She seemed so attractive. He said, "Do you ever have affairs?"

She looked at him, understanding what he meant.

"Yes. Sometimes. Maybe next time we see each other."

"Why not now?" he said.

She went to his hotel room, and he opened a new sexual world for her, as she opened an emotional world for him. After a while the sexual and emotional blended together so the two were hard to tell apart. Both were transformed. Some of the hurt from his failed marriage faded.

She was still giving him ideas about New York when they finished the meal.

"I have to go," she said. "John won't go to sleep until I kiss him good night, and Larry will wonder where I am."

"Sure," Reeder said, feeling the warmth of her presence.

She took his hand before she rose to go. "Have you ever thought about taking up with me again?" she said. "I am not as pinned down as I was now that John is in school."

The thought startled him.

"I.... No. I hadn't thought about it," he said. Mixed feelings surged though him.

She kissed him goodbye and climbed into a taxi, leaving him standing at the curb emotionally confused.

CHAPTER TWELVE

Reeder arrived at the National Science Foundation building a few minutes before 8 o'clock. Kevin Smith had asked to meet with him before the advisory council meeting. The National Science Foundation was housed in a high-rise office building across the street from the World Bank, a few blocks from the White House. NSF shared the building with the Secret Service.

As he entered the building, the security guard sitting at the desk waved him on to the elevators. Considering this building housed the Secret Service, the security was pretty informal, Reeder thought. He took the elevator to the tenth floor and walked to Smith's office. It was too early in the morning for many to have arrived. Most employees were battling traffic into the city.

Smith was at his desk banging away on his machine. Corner offices were highly prized in the bureaucracy and Smith had a good one. Smith waved him to a couch and came from behind the desk to sit with him.

"How are you adjusting?" Reeder asked. Smith had taken the job as head of the evaluation office a few months before, but Reeder had known him a long time.

"Good," he said. "A little more status and power than I am used to. Someone came into my office the other day, stopped dead in his tracks, and asked me where I got that lamp."

Reeder looked at the lamp. It was ugly.

"He said it was an assistant secretary's lamp. Everyone around here is sorted out in rank by office space and furniture, you know."

"Sounds prestigious."

Reeder was trying to sound impressed. He dealt with several bureaucracies, and each had its own personality. The National Science Foundation was a unique blend of bureaucracy and academia. Some staffers were full-time bureaucrats while others were brought from universities on special assignment. Some academics stayed on. Most returned to their universities.

The idea was that close contact with the work being done in universities was critical since NSF funded much of the science, math, and engineering research in the country. Those administering the grants had to be well informed about the latest chemistry or physics if they were to support quality endeavors. Otherwise, the work would be sterile. By all accounts, the NSF had been highly successful and was highly regarded in government and academia.

The organizational culture was a blend of academic seminars and assistant secretarial lamps. After a while, newcomers sank into a Washington world distinct from anywhere else. They called it being inside the Beltway. Or, if one had a bad case of power lust, Potomac fever.

"You do have an opportunity to make a real contribution."

Reeder figured it was politic to flatter Washington bureaucrats in their responsibilities. The disappointments would come soon enough.

"Yes, I would like to establish evaluation as an ongoing enterprise for the Foundation," Smith said. The office was new.

"You would think that an organization dedicated to scientific progress would have embraced evaluation long ago."

"Yes, you would. But that hasn't been the case. The last head of this directorate thought that nothing good could come of evaluation. The organization already enjoyed high prestige and full funding. The director reports to the president, you know. Why mess that up? Only bad things could emerge from evaluations."

"Like Woody Hays and the forward pass. Only three things can happen when you throw a pass, and two of them are bad. Why do it?"

Reeder referred to the former college football coach. Like most American males, Reeder used sports examples to make points. In a country so diverse and politicized, sports talk was a universal language. It established communication with taxi drivers, bartenders, doctors, and senators. Talking politics could get you into dispute. You could depend on sports for common understanding.

"So evaluation has never been given any attention." Smith was going on about the history of the place.

"Why now? What's changed?"

"We have a lot of new money for educational programs, which we didn't particularly want. Congress gave it to us anyhow, over six hundred million dollars. It's the science and math thing, global competition, technology."

"You mean the foundation didn't want the money?"

"Not really. Reagan took us out of the education business. NSF has been interested in scientific research, not education. But Congress doesn't trust the education department. They don't think they are competent. Never has. So they gave us the science and math education money, not them."

Reeder had been around Washington long enough to understand some of the dynamics between Congress and departments. Departments could be on the Congressional shit list for decades. It was easier to get into trouble than get out of it. Bureaucrats knew this, one reason they displayed extreme caution.

"But why evaluation now?"

"Congress wants the new education programs evaluated. They want reports on how the programs are going. They insist."

"How do you like my view?" Smith was looking out the window.

"You can see a bit of the White House from here."

Reeder got up to peer out the window and appear suitably impressed. He could see a corner of the White House from Smith's window.

"Oh, yes, I can see it."

The White House was the center of power. The closer you were to it the better.

Smith switched back to the topic.

"I set up the advisory council to give us advice on evaluating the new programs. I especially wanted you on it."

It was Smith's turn to flatter the academic, knowing how susceptible academics were. Government consultant fees were low, and flattery was a substitute. Smith had been around enough to know how to work the consultants. Reeder knew this too but was flattered nonetheless.

"I'll do my best. Sounds like a good group."

Reeder deflected the compliment, showing appropriate modesty. The men chatted until time for the meeting.

CHAPTER THIRTEEN

Three members of the advisory council were standing around the coffee pot talking. Reeder knew two of them, veterans of the government advisory circuit. He introduced himself to the one he didn't know. Kevin Smith came into the room with a large stack of papers and asked everyone to sit down. The room was standard government issue, bare, no decorations. Sometimes agencies held meetings in hotels since government quarters were crowded and unadorned. Also, being elsewhere got the officials away from their telephones. This meeting was in house.

People sat down at a large rectangle arranged by putting worktables end to end and side to side. They sat where they wanted, staff and advisory members mixed together. Informality among equals was the ethic, if not the fact. Smith started the meeting by asking those present to introduce themselves. He explained that he had formed the committee to provide advice on evaluation. And he had a problem already.

"We understood that we had the evaluation money, about twenty million dollars, to evaluate the NSF math and science education programs. However, Senator Morse has different ideas."

Smith paused and passed a stack of papers around the table. People took the handout and leafed through it while he talked, wondering what they were looking for.

"Senator Morse is chair of the NSF funding committee. A powerful position. She has been a great friend of the foundation. But she has larger ambitions for the evaluation office. She wants us to evaluate *all* the math, science, and engineering education programs in the entire federal government."

He let this statement sink in. No one said anything, wondering what came next.

"In this handout we have estimated how many programs there are across the federal government. I say 'estimated' because no one knows the number for sure."

Reeder knew what Smith meant. The federal government was so huge and sprawling that no one knew what was going on everywhere. Departments pursued their own agendas without much coordination or communication.

"We estimate there are about two-hundred and eighty-five math, science, and engineering education programs. These are spread over about fifteen departments and agencies—NSF, education, defense, commerce, NASA, labor, and so on. Pretty much the full gamut. The total amount of money is about two and a half billion dollars."

Reeder was first to speak as people leafed through the papers.

"How are you going to evaluate all that?"

"Exactly. It's impossible. It would take years, and who knows how much money? We also don't have the staff available to do it."

"Well, not if you were going to do a thorough job."

"And the senator wants the evaluation findings soon." Smith was exasperated. He had an office to establish and an impossible task to perform.

"What are you going to do?" Michael Andrews asked. He was chair of the advisory group. Andrews was from a large private university and had years experience in Washington. He understood the difficulty of the demand and also the pressure to do it.

"I intend stalling her off. Look at our written response to her. It is in the packet we left at your hotel last night."

They fished around in their materials trying to find the document. Some council members needed help.

"We said we would study the situation and come up with a plan to address the topic in a few years."

"She bought that?" Andrews sounded skeptical.

"Yes, she seems to. We haven't heard anything back from her staff. We need time to figure out how to approach the problem. Hopefully, under the next director of this office."

"You don't figure you could do it," Alicia Record said. She was from California and yawning from being three time zones behind.

"It would be a nightmare. We don't have the money to do it and getting the cooperation of the other departments and agencies would be impossible. We don't have any authority over them."

"Isn't this dangerous?" Andrews said. "Ignoring a direct request from a Senator is not the wisest thing to do."

"Our priority is evaluating the NSF programs. Not all the other stuff. That's what we have money to do and what I think we can do."

Smith was firm. Reeder could see Smith's point but he could see Andrews' too. A difficult position to be in. For the most part, advisory councils supported the heads of the offices they were advising. The heads set up the committees and selected the members. On the other hand, advisory members were obligated to give their best advice.

Reeder looked down the list of programs. Hundreds of millions of dollars spread over more than a dozen agencies and departments. No doubt the agencies received their money on the basis of needs expressed by each, without reference to the plans of the others. Evaluators were being asked to make sense of it all, even if it didn't make any sense. Reeder could see Smith's reluctance.

A few more questions and the group moved to the next item on the agenda, examination of an evaluation report completed by an outside contractor. The group broke early for lunch to allow caterers to set up a buffet in the meeting room.

Small talk dominated the lunch break while NSF staffers went to their offices to check their messages. Within the hour Smith returned. He looked ashen. Reeder noticed him as soon as he entered the room. Smith walked over to him.

"The shit has hit the fan!" Smith said, shaken.

"What the matter?"

"Senator Morse. She is threatening to withhold forty million dollars in NSF funds until we conduct the study of the programs she wants evaluated. The director just called me in. He is furious."

Not the way to start a new job, Reeder thought.

"Well, there is a way to do the evaluation quickly. Not very well maybe, but quickly."

"How's that?" Smith was desperate. His confidence had been shaken. Rather than being the assured professional, he looked frightened. Washington had a way of doing that to people. They lived in a closed space.

"You could set up a panel, a blue-ribbon panel, to look into the programs and make a report. It wouldn't be a thorough evaluation but it would provide some findings about these programs fast."

"How long would that take?"

"Four months. Six months. Depends on how fast you move it along."

Smith grasped the idea.

"She wants some indication about how these programs are working, how the money is being spent."

He was talking himself into the idea.

"And you could tell her the blue-ribbon panel was underway. Maybe she would release the money if she figured she would get a report soon."

"How do we go about it?"

"Select some big name scientists and mathematicians. Put a few evaluators on it to make sure it doesn't go awry. The panel can look at programs and whatever information there is. Then the panel can draw some conclusions. Hell, no one knows anything about the programs now. It has to be better than nothing."

Reeder was starting to like the idea himself. He had been on blue-ribbon panels before and had an idea of what they could do. They did have serious deficiencies for sure. They were too superficial. However, this was a desperate situation. He hoped he was giving good advice to his colleague.

"You have to be one of the people on the panel," Smith said, wading in.

"Sure. Ok. I could do that." Looking across federal agencies might be interesting.

Smith went back to his office to make a phone call to the director. He nodded at Reeder when he returned. He settled down the advisory group before telling them the news. The group spent the next two hours talking about how such a panel might work and who would be on it. Smith regained his composure.

CHAPTER FOURTEEN

Reeder caught the afternoon plane back. With the time change, he arrived in time to take a swim. It was a ritual that cleared his head. The locker room in the aquatic center at the university was crowded when he got there. People leaving work to exercise before they went home for the evening. It was not a good time to swim.

He stripped down and took a shower before entering the pool area. All types of male bodies wandered around the locker room naked without concern for modesty. A few had towels wrapped around them. He put on his swimsuit and walked to the pool. The pool was in a large room with a high ceiling. Eight lanes were roped off from each other, each lane twenty-five yards long. As he suspected, the lanes were crowded. He found one with the fewest swimmers and jumped in the water.

He pushed off from the wall as he reached out into the water with his left arm. After a few strokes he fell in rhythm, water gliding past him, cruising along on the surface. This was the good part. On the second lap he overcame the oxygen deficit as his breathing caught up with his activity so the two were in balance. He glided through the water in sync after that. He felt he could swim indefinitely, his muscles practiced to the point of no fatigue. He knew this sense of infinite extension was an illusion. But it was a good feeling.

During the first few laps he thought about whatever problem was on his mind. After a while his thoughts faded out gradually lap by lap. After several laps his thoughts became jumbled, and he concentrated on how many laps he had to swim to finish.

Today New York was on his mind, and women. Both were puzzles he didn't understand. Some laps he thought about New York and how he should proceed with his first report. Other laps he thought about the women in his life, past and present. After more laps in rhythm these ideas faded, and he tried to remember how many laps he had done. Fourteen? Fifteen? He had lost track. He decided to go with the higher number so he had fewer to swim.

He quit when he reached twenty laps, a thousand yards. He took off his goggles, put his hands on the edge of the pool, and hoisted himself from the pool onto the deck, splashing water along the side. He walked back to the locker room barefooted, head down, watching his steps, feeling fatigued in a pleasant way.

He washed the chlorine from his body and hair in the shower as his thoughts returned. At first he was aware of immediate surroundings, the men in the locker room, the noise of men talking and slamming locker doors and flushing toilets. Other thoughts returned. New York, women, what his life might have been, what he needed to do. Big thoughts and little thoughts jumbled together. He dried off and put on his clothes, in no hurry. He went to his car and drove home.

His place was as he left it, books strewn over tables and chairs, clothes hanging where he left them. There was comfort in this. He poured a glass of red wine and looked at his mail. Bills, a consultant check for five hundred dollars. He flipped on the television. Not much happening, and he wasn't interested anyhow. He couldn't get his mind off Elizabeth. He felt like talking to someone. He reached for the phone to see what Neil was doing.

CHAPTER FIFTEEN

Neil was waiting for him at the door. He must have been watching for him out the window. As usual, Neil greeted him warmly, with a chuckle.

"Hey! How are you doing?"

"Good. Good. How are things going for you?"

"Can't complain. How about a drink?"

"Sure. Not too much though."

Reeder was not sure how to introduce the topic of women, though he knew Neil would be interested. No one had more troubled relationships with women than Neil. He had made every mistake in the book. Naturally, people wanted to consult him about such matters. Perhaps they figured however awful their own situation, they couldn't have done worse than Neil. He was in no position to be critical. Another plus was that Neil approached relationship problems with enthusiasm.

"Come by to talk about New York?" Neil asked.

"Not really, though I can always use advice on that. I have some woman problems."

Reeder thought he might as well blurt out what was on his mind. Neil was too astute to pretend it was something else.

Neil stopped pouring whiskey into the glass and turned around to look at Reeder. He was interested enough to stop pouring whiskey.

"I was in Washington and ran into my old flame. Elizabeth. You know the one. From years back."

"Yes, yes."

"I don't know if it was casual or what but she asked if I had ever thought about getting back together with her. I think she was serious."

Neil handed the drink to Reeder and leaned back in a chair.

"What do you think?"

"I'm confused."

Reeder had been honest with Neil about romantic relationships, including the break up of his marriage. At least as honest as he was with anyone. And he had been through many turns with Neil too, in his ups and downs.

"So? What's the problem?"

"She is still married, with a kid. I am not sure I want to get back together with her again. It would be the same old problems, maybe worse."

"So don't."

"That's the problem. She still has allure for me. I feel I am in another world when I am with her. A world of just her and me."

"But then you would have problems again, as in the past. And what if it gets out of hand. What about her kid?"

Reeder had thought about that. What if things got messy and he broke up her family? How would he feel about that? Not good. He came from a broken home. Pushing kids into such situations wasn't the best thing you could do for them.

"Why don't you just give women up like I have?" Neil went on.

"What?"

Reeder was startled. This was the first time he had heard Neil say anything like this. Though Neil was well into his 60s, Reeder knew his penchant for getting involved with women. It was hard to believe he had given them up.

"You've given up women?"

"Yes, I figure I have done enough damage. So I have given them up."

"Since when?"

"A while back. I just haven't talked about it. No need to. I am leading a second-class existence. When you are really in love, that is a first-class existence. But I have lowered my expectations."

Reeder found this difficult to believe. And sad, if true. Few men had paid more attention to women than Neil. And in spite of his plain physical appearance, he was successful with them too. Mainly because of his wit and charm.

"Of course, there is one thing I miss about not having a woman," Neil went on.

"What's that?"

"Not having pressed shirts. No one to iron my shirts for me."

Reeder looked at Neil's face to see if he was serious. He was.

"For Christ sake's. You can't say stuff like that in this day and age."

"Why not? It's true. I can manage the cooking and cleaning and being alone. I just can't press shirts."

Neil was an unreconstructed chauvinist. Reeder knew that. He was a throwback. The good side of his patriarchy was that he took care of people when he was director of the center. Getting contracts, keeping people employed, straightening out personal problems.

The bad side was his attitude towards women, which he never lost after coming to the United States. The attitude was so ingrained that sometimes he didn't realize how people would react to what he said or did. Reeder remembered arguing with Neil over an evaluation report years before. Neil ended the report with, "And aren't all the women in Baltimore pretty?"

Neil was trying to be clever, or, more likely, had a woman in Baltimore he was trying to impress. Reeder had argued with him that he couldn't put that sentiment in a report. Neil ignored the advice and sent the report off. All hell broke loose. The substance of the report was lost in the furor over the closing line. Neil spent months manufacturing acceptable interpretations as to what the line meant. Nothing helped.

Sometimes his advice about women could be helpful, even insightful. When Reeder offended a friend unintentionally, Neil advised him to give her flowers or money.

"That's too obvious!" Reeder said.

"Of course, it's obvious. But it works."

Reeder sent the woman flowers. It worked. The woman treated him as if nothing had happened. It was insights like that, hardly politically correct, that made Neil's advice valuable. Some advice was too strange. When Reeder was split between two women and didn't know what to do, Neil suggested finding a third woman as a way out. That was too bizarre.

Perhaps Neil's daughter, the psychoanalyst, was right to analyze her father. Maybe she was driven to her profession. Neil had a strong influence on others. Would his daughter have insights others didn't, or would they reflect her own problems? Her analysis would make for interesting reading. Neil's mental construction was unlike anyone that Reeder had known.

"Hard to tell you what to do. But I think I would let it alone. It will end in grief again. Either you will be left alone eventually or something worse. I wouldn't get back in. Of course, that's easy for me to say. We aren't talking about my emotions. Or my woman. I've given them up."

Reeder mulled over what Neil was saying, which was what he expected him to say. Neil was probably right. But Elizabeth's pull was strong. He thought what it had been like with her in the old days. A world of their own. For him there was no one else like her. Reeder remained confused with conflicting emotions surging through him. Neil was right about the difference between having a first-class and second-class life. A first-class life meant being deeply in love. There was nothing else like it. It was tempting.

CHAPTER SIXTEEN

Reeder realized that he had work to do whatever personal problems he had. He could not let his personal difficulties prevent him from working. If he had, he would not have accomplished anything in his career. Work was a way to avoid dwelling on what you could not fix in your life.

The New York project was at the top of his list. If he was going to write a report critical of the way the school district was conducting the evaluation, he needed to have a closer inspection of the situation. He needed more information about the evaluation and the program. He arranged another visit to the city.

He flew in during the morning, having scheduled a meeting with the head of the evaluation office later in the day. Were they deliberately committing the errors they were making in the statistical analysis or was it innocent on their part? How he targeted his report depended on that difference.

He took a taxi to Brooklyn and entered the school district building. It looked different during the day, not as sinister. Rick Cole greeted him cordially with a handshake. Cole was short, slender, and balding. They got a cup of the office coffee and sat down to talk, just the two of them.

"Tell me a little about the program. I read the material but I want to make sure I understand how it works."

"Sure. We test the kids in the spring and if they don't get a high enough score, they have to attend summer school. Summer school is eight weeks long, and we have special teachers and materials to increase the test scores."

"How are the teachers trained?"

"In workshops run by the district. Then we test the kids again at the end of summer school. If their scores are not high enough again, they have to repeat the grade they were in."

"Same test?" Reeder watched Cole closely. Cole showed no hesitancy.

"Yes, same test. Then, when they go back to the same grade they go into special classes of no more than twenty students. Special teacher and materials again. We test them once more the next spring."

"Could I observe one of those classes? I'd like to see how they function."

"Sure. No problem. I'll ask the program people to organize a visit for you. Tomorrow?"

"Tomorrow would be good. It's in the summer classes that you are having the greatest test gains so far?"

"Yes, the gains have been phenomenal. Really strong. That's what gives us confidence the program will work, in spite of a lot of skepticism about it."

From what Reeder could tell, Cole was straightforward. No sliding around or evasion about what they were doing or the testing procedures. He did not appear to be a man juggling the numbers. If he was, he was wasting his time in schools. He should be out selling the bridge a few blocks away. Of course, Reeder had been fooled before.

"We don't have the results for the full year. Just for summer school. We don't give the tests until April."

"You do the data analysis in this office?"

"Yes, we have a small group of people who have been doing the reporting on our federal programs for years. I am not a statistician but I have confidence they know what they are doing."

Reeder thought that was possible. Reports sent to Washington to account for federal money were not read. Or else read by those without background to pick up technical flaws. The volume of reports was huge, and no one could process them with facility.

"You had a chance to look at our evaluation plan?" Cole asked.

"Yes, as I mentioned a few weeks ago when I was here, it looks good to me. Except the focus on test scores doesn't leave much room for other program outcomes."

"As I said, no one in the city gives much of a damn about other outcomes. The test scores are what the city has always used to judge schools. That hasn't changed."

"I think you need some other data to balance that out. For example, you might do case studies of some classes to give people a notion of what is happening in classrooms."

"I don't think that will change any minds but I'll bring up the idea with my staff and see what they think. We might be able to do something like that on a small scale. It won't replace the test scores though."

"Yes, I understand that. We also have questions about the data analysis. Whether you have adjusted for regression to the mean. We're not sure about that yet."

Cole was unfazed. "Sure. We are open to any suggestions for improvement you might have about how to analyze the test scores."

"Our concerns are a little technical and we'll put them into our first report and see what you think."

"Ok, good. I'll have to take the issue up with our staff. It may be too technical for me."

They talked for an hour about details of the evaluation plan, the program, and the monitoring by Reeder and his team. Cole was friendly and cooperative. Reeder could detect no hint that the evaluation office was running a scam.

CHAPTER SEVENTEEN

Reeder called Velma Wilson in the Mayor's office during a break, to let her know he was in town. He had not made plans to visit the Mayor's office on this trip. She was busy this afternoon, she said, but asked if he would like to have a drink after work and talk about the project. He said he would.

They met in a bar she suggested at the edge of Greenwich Village. The taxi driver had trouble finding it and circled the block twice. For a moment Reeder thought she had given him the wrong address. But there it was hidden away, a step-down place set below street level. He was fifteen minutes early and had a glass of wine while he waited. He shuddered at the bill. Hell, he could buy a bottle at these prices.

A few people were having drinks before dinner. A fat man in a three-piece suit knocking back martinis, a young woman with the muscular legs of a dancer drinking chardonnay, and a middle-aged couple arguing in low tones at the corner table. Marital problems, Reeder guessed.

He had forgotten how sexy she was until she walked in the door. Shapely legs showing under a black skirt half way up her thigh, her black hair cut around her neck. Exotic. She was tall and full-figured, too big for most men. She suited his taste. She walked straight to him.

"Let a friendly evaluator buy you a drink?" he said.

"That's the idea."

She ordered chardonnay, and they sat down at a small table in the back away from the door. She crossed her legs, exposing a long line of thigh. She knew her legs were her best feature, he figured.

"Is this one of the places you come to often?"

"Yes, one of them. It's not far from where I live."

"In the Village?"

"Near by."

"How are things in the Mayor's office?"

"Good. The polls look great and we are a few days from the election. How are things at the Chancellor's office?"

"Fine. I should have a report to you soon. Looking at their plans and what they have done so far. There might be problems with some of the data analysis they have done."

"What kind of problems?" She was alert to his casual remark. Smart woman.

"I'm not sure at the moment. We have to sort it out. I'll let you know in a few weeks."

He didn't want to explain the problem to her. She would be on the phone to the Chancellor's office wanting to know what was going on. Reeder wasn't ready to back up his criticism yet. He had to get it right and say it the right way. Not a good idea to get people excited without evidence. Let them deal with the problem when the time came, not an idea of a problem.

She sensed there was something more to be said and also that she wasn't going to hear it. He had alerted her to something coming, as he had Cole. That was enough, until he got the message together the way he wanted it. The way in which criticisms were stated was critical. No use going off half-cocked just to impress a sexy woman, tempting though it was. He switched the topic.

"What do you do for entertainment?"

"Plays, movies, restaurants, museums."

"I wish I had something like that where I live. Nothing but cornfields."

"Family?"

"Not any more. Divorced. A couple of almost grown kids."

"I am divorced too. Twice. No kids though."

Good. They had gotten that out of the way. He didn't pursue their marital histories. No use introducing past grief into the discussion. She crossed her legs again, waiting.

"Maybe you might like to take in a play or a museum sometime when I am here for a few days. Or have dinner."

He knew that mixing pleasure with business was a bad idea, especially getting mixed up with clients. It was difficult to deliver hard-hitting evaluations to someone you were sleeping with.

"Yes, I might do that. Not tonight though."

She was interested.

"It must be fascinating working in the Mayor's office."

"You always get to see something new. Sometimes things you don't want to see. But it is interesting, yes. I have been interested in politics since I was in college. Radical politics then."

"Times have changed, haven't they? I didn't think there were many radicals around these days. Everyone is interested in making money."

"You got that right. It makes politicians look altruistic sometimes. If I didn't know better, of course."

"You must still have some idea of social justice if you are involved deeply in politics."

"Yes, I think so. Or else maybe it is just a fascination with power. Being close to the center of power. Sometimes I am not sure myself. The two blend into one another, don't they?"

"I know what you mean. My profession is not immune to such confusion either. There is a strange kind of power in evaluating programs and telling people what's what. Not that you can do anything about it."

"I would think that's a powerful position. Look at us, waiting to see what you say about the Second Chance evaluation."

"Looks more powerful than what it is. The role is pretty limited in many ways." He was flattered that she thought what he did for a living was important, whether it was or not.

"How did you get into it?"

"Accidental. A job came along when I needed one. I got in and never got back out. It's been ok though. Decent pay, interesting projects, and lots of travel. You can't ask for more than that."

He started to say, meeting interesting people too. But that was too obvious. She didn't need someone reading between the lines for her. She was too smart. He didn't want to sound as if he were a traveling salesman passing through town.

"What's your schedule for tomorrow?" She shifted the conversation suddenly. She must have places to go, people to see perhaps.

"Visit a school to see what the program looks like in practice. Talk to a few teachers maybe. Head back in the afternoon."

"Ok, I have to go. Why don't you give me a call in advance next time you come to town? We'll do something if you want."

He walked out the door with her, told her goodbye, and hailed a taxi back to his hotel. She headed off by foot in the opposite direction. He watched her walk down the street as long as he could.

CHAPTER EIGHTEEN

Next morning Reeder grabbed a taxi for Grant Elementary School in midtown Manhattan. Grant had a high percentage of its students in the Second Chance program. Not surprising, since it was located in a poor area of minorities who had not been in the country long. The traffic was thick, and he didn't arrive until after nine-thirty.

Cole had arranged for his visit but Reeder had chosen which school he wanted to see. Grant Elementary was a circa 1900 brick building which had accumulated the dirt of the city over the decades. Grim. It was a tribute to the kids to get up every morning and enter a building like this. No doubt some didn't bother. A security guard at the door escorted him to the principal's office. Inside the corridors were dark but clean. The principal, a short slight man with a bow tie, was expecting him.

"I think you will find Grant an outstanding school in every respect," the principal said. "Outstanding teachers, outstanding students, and high aspirations."

The principal's line, regardless of the school. Did they learn this verbatim in graduate training? After chatting with the principal twenty minutes, Reeder asked if he could see a classroom where someone was teaching failed students.

"Certainly. Mrs. Douglas is one of our finest teachers. Master's degree in English, twenty years in the district, ten years at this school. She has been here as long as I have. She is really dedicated to the students in this neighborhood."

The principal took him to a classroom down the hallway. The teacher looked up when they entered, then went about her business. She was expecting them. The students eyed him up and down. Half were African Americans and half Latinos. A White man in a suit and tie. Nothing new. They went back to what they were doing.

Mrs. Douglas was an African-American, medium height, a little stout, in her 40s. She was standing by her desk in front of the room. She appeared to be starting a lesson. Maybe she had been waiting for his arrival. Hard to say what she had been told in advance of his visit. But he could hardly walk into a school in New York City unannounced. Not these days.

"Now, students, we are going to do some writing today. Take out a piece of paper and a pencil. I want you to write a story about something that happened to you recently."

Students scrambled around in their desks and backpacks looking for paper and pencils. Mrs. Douglas waited.

When all was quiet she said, "Now think of a story about what happened to you and write it down on paper."

A fidgety boy in the front row waved his hand around to get her attention. He must be hard to handle all day.

"Yes, George."

"Mrs. Douglas, I can't think of anything to write about."

"What happened today before you came to school, George?"

"My mom got me up and got my little brother up. Then we ate some cereal and watched TV. Then I walked to school. When I got to the corner some boys put a kitten down some stairs with a grate over the top. It couldn't get out. It was meowing. They left it there and I got a stick and tried to get it out. But I couldn't do it. Another boy came along and helped me and we got it out. And I came to school."

"That's good, George. Why don't you write that down just like you told the story?"

George picked up his pencil and scribbled on the paper in large block letters. Reeder liked the way Mrs. Douglas handled the assignment. Other students were writing or talking to one another. Mrs. Douglas walked around the room stopping to see what each student was doing. Reeder wondered what the finished papers would look like. After half an hour he left the classroom and walked back to the principal's office.

The classroom had the right number of students. Fewer than twenty, and the teacher seemed competent. Reeder was impressed. He wondered what putting students who had failed together in one room did to their ideas about themselves. Did other students make fun of them?

Reeder remembered his own elementary school long ago. Being humiliated for poor handwriting and missed assignments. The name-calling. Kids could be cruel to one another. Was George's concern about the kitten concern about himself? That was pushing things. There were things you could see in a classroom but most things you couldn't, especially the important thoughts going on in kids' minds.

CHAPTER NINETEEN

Reeder asked the principal if he could talk to some teachers during their free period. Maybe he could get a feel for the program from them. The principal was hesitant. He hadn't prepared for this. Reeder figured Mrs. Douglas was his best teacher. Letting Reeder talk to other teachers in the school without preparation was chancy. Yet here was this man authorized by 110 Livingston Street to visit. The principal didn't understand what the man was doing, other than something to do with the Second Chance program.

Reeder had not told the central office that he wanted to talk to teachers. He knew the school would prepare the classroom visit, give him their best shot. He would get better information off the cuff, unrehearsed. He took the chance that the principal would let him interview teachers. Reeder's ambiguous authority, backed by the central office, worked in his favor. Principals and teachers were used to complying with things they didn't understand.

"I could assemble a few teachers who teach in the program during the third hour. They have it free for a planning period together."

"Great," Reeder said. "That would work fine. I want to get their views about how the program is going."

The principal looked uneasy, though Reeder tried to make his interest sound benign.

He met the teachers in the teachers' coffee lounge. Mrs. Douglas was there, along with an African American man her age and two White teachers in their 50s, one dumpy and one thin. The African American man was dressed in a suit and tie. The other two were casual, no ties. Reeder poured a cup of coffee from the pot, black stuff that had been around all day, and sat down with them at a table.

"I am working with the Chancellor's office and want to ask you a few questions about the Second Chance program." He knew they wouldn't understand the circumstances regarding the evaluation. To them it was all chaos in the central office.

"How do you think the program is going?"

After some hesitation, Mrs. Douglas spoke. "Some students are doing very well. And some not so well. I don't know how this will translate into improved test scores. I think they are learning though."

The dumpy White man in his 50s came in quickly.

"We do the best we can with these students. I don't know what more we can do with them. If 110 Livingston Street thinks they can do better, let them come here and teach them. It's not that easy."

The thin White teacher supported his companion.

"These kids stay up half the night watching TV. Their mothers don't discipline them. Their fathers are gone. It's hard to hold their attention. A lot of them don't even speak English. We just baby sit a lot of the time."

The Black man didn't like the way the discussion was heading.

"These students have problems at home but most come to school and try to do their best."

"Which is none too good." The White teacher with the gut wasn't having any. "You take marginal students, put them in one classroom, you can't expect much."

Mrs. Douglas was upset by these remarks. "These students can do as well as any if they are given a chance. No one has given them a chance."

"You can say that. I have been teaching these kinds of students for thirty years. Longer than you've been here. It's hopeless really. Most will never get through high school." The dumpy teacher thought he had an audience in Reeder, someone with a line to the central office.

Reeder tried to redirect the discussion back to the program. "Don't you think these kids can do all right if they have the extra help the program provides?"

"I don't think these kids even belong in school, many of them. Thirty years ago they wouldn't have been in school. Or even in the city. Or even in the country. Now we have to try and teach students who don't belong here."

The dumpy man was using the opportunity to vent his frustrations. The thin man elaborated.

"Fred expresses it more strongly than I would. I have been teaching these kids about as long as Fred has. Most just don't have the ability to do academic work. That's the long and the short of it. We are talking about mental ability here. They are going to do the grunt work of the society. Or worse."

Reeder realized he was dealing with alienated teachers, not unusual. Schools and teachers were pounded by the media and politicians daily. They had become scapegoats for society's ills. He wondered why these men were teaching in the program at all.

"Why did you volunteer to teach in the Second Chance program?"

"Who volunteered?" the dumpy teacher said. "The principal needed somebody to teach the classes. He told me I was it. I sure as hell didn't volunteer. I just wanted to keep my job."

"I thought the teachers were supposed to volunteer, to do the job willingly."

"I volunteered," Mrs. Douglas said.

"So did I," the Black man said. "More or less."

The thin White teacher said nothing. Reeder wasn't surprised by the clumsy implementation of the program. He was taken aback by the bitterness the two teachers expressed. They hardly seemed good choices for teaching minority students since they had no faith in the students' abilities. And perhaps harbored worse feelings about their race.

"Why not do something else if you don't like the job you are doing?" Reeder was blunt, blunter than he should have been.

The rule of interviewing was not to lead the person being questioned improperly. People would tell you what they thought you wanted to hear if they could figure out what it was. This was the secret ingredient of media talk shows. No good if you wanted accurate information. Reeder admonished himself. The men's frustration was seeping into his own behavior.

"I have five more years to go to retirement," the dumpy man said. "Five more years, and I'm outta here!"

"It's difficult to find jobs at our age," the thin man said. "I used to think I would like to be a principal. Maybe work my way up in the district. I took administration courses at night and during the summer. And got a master's degree. But they never gave me a chance."

The other two remained silent during this exchange. Resigned perhaps. They had heard these comments before. Did they feel resentful towards their fellow teachers?

Reeder asked questions about the curriculum materials and the training the teachers received. He had little time. The period was over and the teachers hurried back to their classrooms. He wondered how many embittered teachers there were in city classrooms. How many people who had wanted to work their way up in the system who felt trapped in classrooms with kids they didn't like. Who turned their bitterness against their students. He sensed the challenges the schools were up against. It made the Chancellor's strong actions understandable.

CHAPTER TWENTY

The flight back was uneventful. Reeder had a glass of wine on the plane and picked at the food, something he couldn't recognize in a red sauce. At least he had a seat between him and the next passenger. He inclined the seat back and closed his eyes, listening to the noise of the engines.

The interview with the teachers had given him more than he bargained for. That was usually the case. You went into the field to look at a program and discovered things you hadn't thought about when imagining it. Programs were implemented by people who had their own motivations. Their agendas often had little to do with the plans on the drawing board. It was a good idea to take a close look at what you were evaluating, even if you didn't know what you were looking for. If you put yourself in the right situation, reality had a way of hitting you in the face.

But what could he do about the teachers? What difference would that make? The district cared about test scores. Nothing else. Discovering the schools had embittered teachers wouldn't change the test results. The central office knew they had an unhappy work force. Or did they? What could they do about it if they did?

There was also Mrs. Douglas, doing an excellent job in her classroom in spite of the problems. How many teachers were like her and how many like the other two? Reeder imagined thousands of teachers across the city doing their jobs as best they could, grousing to their spouses, but not complaining about their station in life or the difficulties of their jobs. Heroic in a way, though no doubt they didn't see themselves like that.

He could also see why the older men might become embittered after years of teaching. Teaching was not a career for ambitious people. After years of struggling in the classroom, subject to insensitive administrators who made the work more difficult, stinging from daily criticisms of the schools in the press, you might wonder why you got into a profession with such poor pay and lack of respect.

Reeder tossed the ideas around in his mind. He knew that he had to write a report that rejected the test gains the district had been claiming. Perhaps he could balance the report with a portrait of Mrs. Douglas's classroom to provide encouragement that good things were happening, even if the test gains were not there yet. That would not make the district administrators happy but maybe that was the best he could do.

A light rain had fallen in temperatures below freezing. Fortunately, the landing strip was clear. The plane landed and he walked carefully to his car, slipping on the ice repeatedly but catching his balance. The car was covered with a thin sheet of ice. He scrapped it off as best he could and drove home carefully on slippery roads. Ice coated trees, telephone poles, and power lines, even stop signs. His car slid when he put on the brakes. He pushed the brake pedal gently trying to shorten the slides. Each stop was a challenge. He reached his house by driving twenty miles an hour.

Inside everything looked as he left it. At least the lights were working, a problem in freezing rainstorms. As he took off his coat, he noticed the three volumes of Proust. He had taken on the task of reading the whole work this winter and still had half a volume to go. He was too tired tonight, though it would be a good night for reading in bed. He flipped through the TV channels trying to find some news.

His mind slipped back to Velma in New York. And to Elizabeth. Where was that going? Where was either relationship going? Did he want to become involved with Elizabeth again after all these years? It had been incredible once. But try it again? He felt conflicted. Velma had been divorced twice. Was she hard to get along with? Something wrong with her? She was certainly sexy.

He found news about the stock market on CNN. The market had dropped sharply again today. He listened to the analysts talk to each other. They didn't seem to know any more than he did. He wondered if his work was similar, pretending to provide answers to questions that people wanted to know about. Clients listened even when you didn't know more than the financial analysts. Maybe the knowledge he provided was as faulty.

He left his mail untouched and went to bed. As he drifted off to sleep, he wondered whether he should sell some stocks. He played with the numbers in his head until he couldn't remember anything.

CHAPTER TWENTY-ONE

Reeder rose early next morning and was in the office by seven. He needed a clear head and no interruptions to write the New York report. He figured it should be short, no more than ten pages. People in the Mayor and Chancellor's offices didn't have time to read long documents.

The blend of the technical and nontechnical was tricky. He had technical readers in the evaluation personnel but nontechnical ones in the political offices. And he had a difficult topic, the mistaken test gains due to regression. He would have to strike a balance in making the report readable for the nontechnical readers while making it authoritative for those who could understand the test score analysis.

How positive and how negative should he be? The message was that the test score gains were nonexistent. That message alone was too negative. He could balance that conclusion with an assessment of the evaluation plan the district had developed, which was not bad, and throw in a reference to Mrs. Douglas's class to provide hope that things might improve.

This tact might prove to be too positive if no gains in test scores developed but no one knew at this time. Simply because there were no gains during the summer didn't mean there would be none during the academic year when students had more time in Second Chance classes.

Reeder thought about his report as he drove to the office. Once he had a cup of coffee in hand, he fired up his computer. He jotted down five topics he wanted to cover—an introduction that set the tone, a review of the plan, a challenge to the test gains, a look at Mrs. Douglas's classroom, and suggestions to strengthen the evaluation design. He took a sip of coffee and plunged ahead. He wrote quickly, knowing he could backtrack. The first task was to get the ideas down.

He worked steadily for two hours, pausing to think for a few minutes at a time, then jotting down more ideas. It was easy until he got to the regression. He thought of ways to convey the concept that would be meaningful for those who didn't understand tests. When he bogged down, he got up from his desk and poured another coffee from the pot in the seminar room. He was getting himself wired with caffeine.

In two hours he had seven pages. Now for revision. He went back to the beginning to read the report through for flow and clarity. He rewrote sentences, replaced words, and moved phrases to the front or back of sentences to make references clear. He noticed spots where he jumped from one thought to another abruptly. He added connections between sections.

An interesting thing about writing was that he never knew exactly what he was going to say until he wrote it. He worked from a brief outline, a few phrases placed at the beginning of the document, at least with a paper this short. Usually he was surprised by what he had said when he was done.

For this report he invented examples to explain the regression effect. To improve the evaluation design, he suggested doing case studies, like Mrs. Douglas's class, in which others could see the program functioning. By the time he finished he had eight pages.

He read back through the document looking at each word carefully. He knew from sorrowful experience that readers could bounce off the wall by catching the nuance of a single wrong word. Words that attributed bad motives to people were explosive. People felt their worth was being examined, and they could hardly take comments impersonally. Usually he could catch trip words before he sent the report. Sometimes he couldn't and found them only from negative reactions. He wanted readers to focus on the ideas he wanted to convey, not on misunderstandings.

As he finished, Reeder was pleased with the way it looked. There were two points he wasn't sure about. He wasn't sure if he had compromised the regression explanation too much, and he wasn't sure what to say about minorities. He would discuss these with his team. If you were working with a team, it was a good idea to allow them to make contributions.

By the time he finished and leaned back in his chair, it was nearly eleven. He had been lucky that he had no interruptions. A good morning's work. Maybe the New York project would go smoothly after all. He sent an e-mail to his colleagues to arrange a meeting, attaching an electronic copy of the draft to the message. Time for a swim.

CHAPTER TWENTY-TWO

Next morning Reeder walked across campus to the administration building for a meeting of the Vice-Chancellor's promotion and tenure committee. It had warmed up and the sun was shining across the flat fields. Hundreds of students hurried between classes, their coats thrown open to the thaw.

He reached the meeting room before anyone else, a room dominated by a long table. The promotion and tenure committee was more serious than the faculty meetings. If assistant professors were not promoted, they were forced to leave the university. They lost their jobs, with the humiliation and blow to their careers that entailed. They had seven years in which to achieve promotion.

The committee was chaired by the Vice-Chancellor and appointed from departments across the university. Committee members were leading professors on campus. Unlike faculty meetings that served as platforms for display, there was little showmanship in the promotion work. It was too serious. Careers hung in the balance.

Reeder fingered through the files in front of him. Information on six professors up for promotion. They came from different departments, and each candidate had a voluminous folder of materials—lists of publications, references from authorities in their fields, student ratings of their classes, descriptions of services they performed, and lists of research grants they had received. The committee's task was to review these materials and vote on whether the candidates deserved promotion.

The Vice-Chancellor entered the room and greeted Reeder. Bruce Montclair was medium height, dark haired, personable, bright, former head of the physics department. Being VC was the toughest job on campus. He had to contend with departments competing for resources and yet maintain good relations with them. He had to be an SOB and make them like it, part of the ethic of collegial relationships. Most people didn't stay in the job long. This VC also had a sense of humor. Not a requirement.

"You in town for a few days?" he said, referring to Reeder's extensive travel. Montclair sat down at the head of the long conference table and poured himself a cup of coffee from the pot on the side.

Reeder grinned. "Thought I would see what the weather was like. If it doesn't warm up soon, I may have to leave again."

"Where have you been?"

"New York. Washington."

Reeder briefed Montclair on the New York project in a few sentences. The Vice-Chancellor liked to know what his faculty did. He didn't want to know too much. With fifteen hundred faculty members it was difficult to remember names and faces, let alone activities. He needed enough information to tell others what was happening on campus and to maintain good relations with the faculty. It was a requirement of his job that he pretended to know what was going on, even if he didn't. Otherwise, he looked ineffective.

Montclair listened as other committee members filed into the room. Reeder could tell he was pleased about the project. He liked the university's name bandied about in New York. It made the university faculty look important and sought after. At the same time the jibe about being on campus was no joke. Students rebelled against professors who missed classes. Balancing research activities and teaching obligations was a struggle.

At 10 o'clock precisely Montclair started the meeting. He expected people to be there. Although he chaired the meeting, he didn't comment about the candidates. At least he wasn't supposed to. The committee was advisory to him. He listened to the arguments and arrived at his own conclusions. Ultimately, he made the decision to recommend for or against promotion based on committee discussions. However, it was rare for him to go against committee recommendations. Out of a hundred cases a year, he reversed the committee's judgment only a few times.

Montclair and eight faculty members were seated around the table. Two were missing. The first case was a history professor up for promotion and tenure. Jack Philips, from the English department, presented the case. He had a slight accent left over from North Carolina.

"Professor Bromwell has an excellent teaching record. She has high student ratings and an enviable record serving on university committees, particularly those dealing with gender issues. However, she has only one book and one published article. The book is on feminist activity in New England between 1900 and suffrage. The article is derived from that work and is in a leading history journal. There is no question that her teaching is good enough. And her service in committee work. But is one book and one article in seven years enough?"

Philips left it open but it was clear he had doubts. The criteria for promotion were research, teaching, and service. Research meant publications in journals, teaching meant handling students competently, and service meant serving on university and professional committees. How many publications did you need? It varied from field to field. The standards for meeting the criteria were open to interpretation.

The other person assigned to present the case, Helen Moore from philosophy, took her turn.

"I agree with Jack about the teaching. As to publications, the book has been reviewed well in two journals. We have the reviews. I think she deserves promotion."

Frank Eagleton, from electrical engineering, entered the discussion. "One book in seven years doesn't seem like much to me. It's probably her dissertation study."

Different disciplines had different publication outlets. Scientists and engineers published articles in journals, rarely books. And in a research university they were expected to publish several articles a year. One book in seven years made no sense to them.

"Historians publish books mostly, and they work a long time on each one," Moore said.

She was arguing for the candidate's record. No one said anything explicitly, but there was a gender issue. The women on the committee defended female candidates. Some of the men were more negative about both male and female candidates. Philips was one of the hard liners.

"It seems to me we should have more reviews of the book before we make a case for promotion. Two reviews are not many."

"Yes, but her outside references are very good also," Helen Moore said.

Six historians around the country had written positive letters about the candidate's work. Trouble was, most reference letters were positive, as everyone knew. Years before, when documents were kept confidential, some reference letters were negative. Now few scholars risked sending negative assessments for fear they would be subject to legal action. That made judging the quality of the references difficult.

Philips was polite but persistent. "Did you notice the letter from the man from Yale? He said her work ranked 'well above average' among her peers. I think the phrase is in his conclusion on the second page."

"Well, what does that really mean?" Moore said. "Most of his letter is very positive, particularly the parts describing details of her work. Her work is 'thorough, original, and a substantial contribution to the area.' That sounds positive to me."

Reeder didn't say anything. His reading of the case was that the woman was all right. Not outstanding but all right. He understood Philip's reluctance to grant tenure to a mediocre scholar. But most people awarded tenure were not outstanding. This historian's record was no worse than most.

The discussion about the details of the candidate's record went on for thirty minutes. The argument was mostly between Philips and Moore, with two others asking questions. Finally, the VC had heard enough and called for a vote. The vote was six for promotion and two against, with two absent. Harrington, from biology, voted with Philips, as usual. Reeder voted with the majority.

The Vice-Chancellor suggested they take a break. They had a difficult case coming up. Three of the men headed for the toilet two floors down.

CHAPTER TWENTY-THREE

The committee members sat down quickly when the VC called the meeting back to order.

"We have a difficult case before us. An unusual case."

Reeder looked at the VC. Montclair looked glum. This case was not to his liking.

"We received the file you have on Michael Skinner the way you have it before you. Then we received this a week ago. I don't need to remind you that you are pledged to confidentiality in these meetings."

He opened a large manila envelope, pulled out a set of photographs, and slid them before the committee so they could see the photos. They appeared to be of relics of some kind, shards of pottery. Philips picked up two photos, looked at Montclair and shrugged his shoulders.

Montclair cleared his throat as if he had to make an effort to speak.

"Skinner is up for promotion in archeology. These photos are supposed to be of artifacts he discovered on Indian digs in Arizona. According to the letter we received in this packet from two of his colleagues, he gets drunk on these digs, sets up the artifacts as targets, and throws beer bottles at them. He has destroyed some."

The group was stunned. No one said anything. Finally, Reeder spoke.

"These are supposed to be photos of the artifacts he has destroyed?"

"Yes, exactly. Photographic evidence collected by his colleagues."

"How do we know they are authentic?"

"We have the written, signed testimony of the two people who took the photos here in this letter."

People were struggling with their thoughts as they sorted through the photos. Reeder picked up the letter and read it carefully. There were additional allegations.

Reeder turned back to Montclair. "What does Skinner say about all this? Where is his response?"

"We don't have it. His colleagues haven't told him they've filed this complaint."

"They haven't confronted him about this stuff?"

"No."

"Have you talked to them?"

"Not yet. I wanted to see what this committee thought before we took any further steps. This is formally part of the promotion process. It is important to follow procedures."

Reeder looked across the table at Philips, who was looking at him at the same time. They recognized what a mess this could be. The situation was unbelievable. Things like this didn't happen in universities.

"There are other charges in this letter too," Reeder said.

"Yes, that when he gets drunk he hits on the female students and has slept with some," Montclair said.

"He wouldn't be the first professor who did that," Philips said.

"That doesn't make it right!" Helen Moore jumped in. "We have policies about that kind of behavior!"

"What about his regular file? What does his teaching and publishing record look like?"

"It's pretty good," Montclair said. "Normally, I judge he would have little trouble securing promotion. Lots of publications in respectable journals, student ratings that are ok—not great, but ok—and normal activity on committees."

"Except for the little fact that he gets drunk on digs and uses Native artifacts as targets." Reeder couldn't resist the comment.

Montclair managed a weak smile. "Yes, well, maybe. We don't know his side of the story. The point is, what do we do with these photos? They were unsolicited and not part of the normal review process. Skinner doesn't know they exist."

"The first thing," Reeder said, "is that we need to confront him with these accusations and get his side of the story."

"We don't have any formal procedures for that," Montclair said. "In the rules we only have the option of asking the department for more information. We have nothing in the rules about soliciting the opinion of a candidate."

"Yeah, well, we don't have anything in the rules about receiving this kind of information either," Philips said. "Yet, here it is."

"That's one way out," Franklin Ellis from psychology said. "We received these photos through improper channels. We could dismiss the information as being outside the proper channels of communication."

Reeder, Philips, and Moore looked at Ellis with disdain. Ellis always tried to avoid sticky problems. He was interested in getting on with his own work, which was substantial.

"No," Reeder said. "I would rather be able to live with myself."

Reeder's remark was too sharp to a fellow committee member. Montclair rushed in to prevent an angry exchange. He had enough problems without dissension on the committee. He looked at Reeder.

"What are you suggesting?"

"I am suggesting we show Skinner the photos and the accusations against him and give him a chance to respond."

"Yes," Philips said. "That's a good idea. Let's hear what he has to say. We need his side of the story before we can take action. We don't know enough. Anyone has a right to answer personal charges. Even in a university."

"I agree," Moore said. "We need to get his side of the story. Maybe these charges are fabricated. Maybe some of his colleagues are out to get him. I hear he is not popular in his department."

Montclair looked around the table to see if anyone had other opinions. No one said anything. With Philips, Moore, and Reeder lined up on one side, their position was likely to carry the committee. Others were happy to extricate themselves however they could. The prospect of having to decide what to do in such a case was horrific. They would have to go on record. They could imagine lawsuits.

"Ok, let's vote," said Montclair.

The vote was eight to nothing, with two members absent. The time for the meeting had run out. Committee members had enough for one day.

"I will handle this as confidentially and as delicately as I can," Montclair said. "I remind you that this is confidential and that we will have the newspapers all over us if word gets out. Not to mention a dozen lawyers."

The committee left it with Montclair to request more information, which was probably the way the Vice-Chancellor had wanted it from the beginning, Reeder figured. What a mess.

CHAPTER TWENTY-FOUR

Reeder walked to the swimming pool slowly, thinking about the meeting. What a bizarre case. He was at the point where he thought he had seen everything but something crazy always popped up. Maybe life was like that. It was not clear what the resolution of this case could be since it didn't fit the rules of university promotion. That was for sure.

Students filled the campus walks heading off to lunch. Reeder zigzagged through them trying not to get run over by fast cyclists, who should not have been on the walks but were there anyhow. The pool was crowded at lunchtime but he found an open lane. His thoughts about the strange situation with the artifacts dwindled away with each lap until he was trying to remember how many more laps he had to swim.

He had arranged a meeting with his team on the New York project at two. The other three drifted into the small conference room one at a time. Reeder opened the meeting to discuss the draft report he had written.

"What do you think about this draft of the report?"

"I think it is well written," Winslow said.

It was rare to start a meeting with criticism. Always say something good first, even if it was an effort. In general, people could take less honest evaluation than they thought they could, even evaluators. Academics developed tact by dealing with students over the years. They handled each other with even more tact. Reeder recognized the move and waited for what else Winslow had to say about the report.

"However there is a small problem with the way you have phrased the regression analysis," Winslow continued. "The example you use here is not quite correct. It might mislead readers."

"Yes, I recognized it as a stretch when I wrote it. But we are dealing with an arcane technical issue. I thought I had to give them something to hang the idea on. Give them a chance for some intuitive understanding. Otherwise they are left with only our word and some numbers."

"I realize that. You are right, of course. But if you carry your analogy too far, it becomes ludicrous. It's like Auden's poem comparing W. B. Yeats body to a great city, body part by body part. Pretty soon you start to wonder where the sewage system is."

Winslow was a surprise sometimes. Lost in his great technical mind of numbers, you were amazed he had even heard of Yeats or Auden. But he had a point. Maybe Reeder had pushed the analogy too far. He could end up having to explain where his analogy did not apply. That would defeat his intent of making the report accessible.

"I see your point. But I hate to give up explaining the regression concept altogether. Do you have ideas about how to present it?"

"Actually, I don't think your analogy is a bad one. If we tweak it a bit I think it might be acceptable. I made some notes on my copy. I'll give it to you after the meeting."

"Ok. Great. That would be very helpful."

Winslow was willing to compromise to make the report comprehensible. That would help. The other two remained silent during the exchange between Winslow and Reeder. The issue was outside their expertise, and Reeder was the leader of the project and author of the report. It was up to him to reach an understanding with each of them. He had the final say but he had to respond to their opinions for the benefit of having their names on it.

"Other issues?"

"I don't think there is enough emphasis on racial issues in the evaluation plan." Garcia was speaking. "I know you mention this in your review of the plan but it still is not enough, in my opinion."

Reeder had not had a chance to mention his meeting with the embittered teachers at Grant Elementary School. His sense that some of their attitude was racial was based on his gut feeling. It was better not to make accusations he had no way of proving. He thought that something more should be included in the plan to get at this aspect. Better that it originate from Garcia.

"What do you have in mind?"

"I was thinking the district could do extensive racial and ethnic breakdowns of the findings. You know, African Americans, Hispanics. We talked about this before. Also, the case studies you recommend could look at the ethnic issues."

"I suggested that to the school district, the racial breakdown, but they seemed resistant. However, I agree with you that something is needed. I will emphasize this in my revision. Any one object?"

Winslow and Rusk shook their heads.

"I am not sure how to make race a focus of the case studies. Let me think about it. If we become too overt we might insult them."

"I would rather insult them than have the issue swept under the rug."

"You have a point. I'll put it in the report but leave the question open about how it is managed. Let's think about it and make some suggestions later. I'll count on you for ideas."

"Ok, I'll think about it too."

"Any other ideas about the report?"

"I don't think the reading focus is strong enough," Rusk said.

Reading was Rusk's area of expertise and a focus of the Second Chance Program. That was why Reeder had chosen him for the team.

"What do you suggest?"

"You don't make enough out of the difference between methods for teaching reading. We have the 'whole language' approach and the 'phonics' approach. There has been an enormous amount of research comparing these. Yet their evaluation plan says nothing about the research, and you don't mention it in your draft." Rusk sounded prickly.

"I realize there is a huge controversy and lots written about different approaches. I also realize the contest between approaches is intense. But how much can we bring into the evaluation and how much can we say about it in our report?"

"We could say that the research evidence suggests that the 'whole language' approach is superior for teaching students to read and write in the long run." Rusk was an advocate of whole language teaching.

"Yes, but the literature is huge. How much can we drag in? We could devote our entire report to the issue and barely scratch the surface."

"I think we have to take a stand. They are veering towards phonics in the Second Chance program, given the materials I have seen."

"Yes, Walter, I understand. But I don't think it's a good idea to make that the focus of the evaluation. Or of our report. The Second Chance program is about retention, flunking kids, making them repeat a grade."

"But the reading controversy is involved too!"

"I realize that. And I understand how strongly you feel about the issue. However, to make the issue the main one is to miscast the evaluation, in my opinion. What about this? What if I put in a few paragraphs discussing the issue but not insist they make it part of their evaluation? We could draw attention to the issue without making them refocus."

Rusk was not happy with this compromise. He looked sullen. Reeder knew that introducing a huge research literature on the methods of teaching reading into the evaluation was difficult. The literature was relevant up to a point but where did you draw the line? Second, the main policy issue was flunking kids, not teaching methods. They should not recast the focus away from what New York was doing with the Second Chance Program. Some things were more relevant and some less so.

"I guess I can live with that." Rusk said. He slouched down in his chair.

Reeder left it at that. Not everybody was going to be happy. "Ok, I'll revise the report and send it off. I'll e-mail you a copy of the final draft, of course."

He went back to his office and started on the revisions while the discussion with the team was fresh in his mind. He looked at the notes each had made on the draft and accepted most of their editorial suggestions. He rewrote the regression section to comply with what Winslow wanted and elaborated the race issue. He added two paragraphs on teaching methods of reading but did not recommend revising the evaluation.

He finished in two hours and read the report over. He was satisfied. Should he e-mail it to them or send it by surface mail. Considering how sensitive they seemed to be about confidentiality, perhaps he had better send it by surface mail. He typed "CONFIDENTIAL" on the first page and ran off two copies. He mailed one copy to the Mayor's office and one to the Chancellor's office. No spare copies floating around New York. He wondered how the people there would react.

CHAPTER TWENTY-FIVE

Reeder sat in his office looking out the window. The ground was wet and muddy from the thaw. It had been two weeks since he sent the report to New York. He had heard nothing, as if the report didn't exist. What did that mean? It took bureaucracies a long time to formulate responses. Layers of administrators to consult. Was he feeling anxious about nothing?

He settled back in his chair and resumed reading student papers. This was a rough part of teaching, trying to maintain interest in what students were writing. Occasionally, a student said something interesting, something you hadn't thought about. For the most part the ideas were the same, nothing new. Grading the papers was one of the worse tasks of teaching.

A knock on his office door. It was Thomas Pickering, a student from the master's class. Pickering was short, squat, and wore a crew cut from the 1950s. Reeder didn't like the man. He was surly and sneaky, in Reeder's opinion. Perhaps he reminded Reeder of someone.

"What can I do for you, Tom?" He motioned the student to sit in the chair next to the desk.

"I think you have given me a lower grade on this last paper than I deserve."

Reeder looked at him. This problem again? He had been through this with the man before.

"I told you. It is a figment of your imagination. I grade you the same as I grade everyone else." He didn't admit to the student that he did not like him. The student sensed it.

"You see this last paper?" Pickering said.

"Yes, I see it. I gave those papers back last week."

"You gave me a 'B' grade on it."

"That's what it deserved."

"You gave Valverde an 'A'."

"That's what he deserved."

"Yes, but I copied Valverde's paper word for word. You gave him an 'A' and me a 'B.' Here's his paper."

What was this? Reeder took Valverde's paper and compared it to Pickering's. They were the same, word for word. Reeder didn't know what to say. The student had him cold. What was worse than giving them different grades for the same paper, Reeder had not realized that he had read two papers exactly the same. It demonstrated what little attention he paid while he graded papers. He was chagrined.

Reeder thought about chastising the student for cheating. That would be a cheap shot though. Not even Pickering deserved that. Without saying a word, he took a red pen from on top his desk, marked out the grade "B", and substituted a big "A" on the paper. Pickering snickered as he left the office without thanking him. He had proved his point.

Reeder sat at his desk thinking about the incident. He had deceived himself. Knowing that he didn't like the student, he still thought he could appraise the man's work fairly. Self-delusion. The truth was that grading was more subjective than teachers believed, even if the subjectivity of grades was no secret to students. He recalled the scandal in the sociology department when the faculty gave the same exams to their Master and PhD students, thinking they could distinguish between master and doctoral performance without knowing whose paper it was. He had warned them they couldn't tell the difference. Of course, they failed many of their doctoral students and gave some of the master's students doctoral passes. A fiasco.

Reeder pondered whether he should have students put identification numbers on their papers rather than names. He could grade papers without knowing who was who and look up names from a code sheet after grades were assigned. He wondered how students would react to such a procedure. They might resent the impersonality. Earlier in his teaching he gave objective tests, fill in blanks. Graduate students hated it. He abandoned objective testing after strenuous student protest, though the papers were easy to mark and assignment of grades was consistent. Students wanted to write essays that expressed their originality. Unfortunately, their papers came out with the same ideas class after class.

Reeder ruminated on these experiences as his mind drifted off the paper he was reading. He started reading the paper again, for the third time. The phone rang, a welcome relief.

"Hello, Professor Reeder? This is Sam Kepner from the Chancellor's office, New York City. How are you?"

"Good. How are you, Sam? Did you get my report?"

"Yes, we got it." A pause. "The Chancellor's mad as hell! I just had it out with him in his office. He's fuming!"

"He didn't like the report?" This was obvious but Reeder didn't know what else to say.

"He is yelling, 'Goddamn professors! You try to do something and they fuck you up! They never do anything useful, just criticize other people!'"

"I didn't think the report was that negative. We had some positive things in it." His response sounded weak.

"Not according to him. He is angry. I tried to reason with him, saying it's only the first report. He wouldn't listen. I can't calm him down. I think the best thing to do is for you and him to sit down across the table from each other and have it out between the two of you. You explain to him what you are saying and why. I can't do anything with him!"

"Yes, I could do that." Reeder was surprised. He expected the district to be unhappy with the report, given that he was challenging the test gains, gains the Mayor used in his electoral campaign. He didn't expect a reaction as strong as this, though he knew the stakes were high.

"How soon can you get here?" Kepner was not giving him any choice, though he pretended to ask. Reeder was being called on the carpet. The Chancellor's office had its own way of dealing with dissidents. These were not novices.

"Depends. You want me to bring some members of my team along?" He was thinking of Winslow, who would be the authority on the test scores if that was the burr. "If so, I will have to see when they are available."

"No, no. We want you. Right away. You and the Chancellor can have this out between you. Just you two across the table from one another." He made it sound like a duel.

"I teach class tomorrow. How about the day after? It'll cost you a high priced plane ticket though."

"Don't worry about that. The cost. That's the least of our worries right now. Day after tomorrow. You call back and leave the details with my secretary when you make your travel arrangements. I'll tell the Chancellor. He's waiting."

Kepner hung up without waiting for a response.

Reeder was suddenly alert, adrenalin pumping, pulse up. Well, he thought, at least they have taken the report seriously. I can't complain about that. He felt uneasy about the confrontation that lay ahead. Was he in over his head? Without waiting for an answer, he reached for the phone to make travel arrangements to go to New York.

CHAPTER TWENTY-SIX

Reeder arrived in New York early in the evening. It was rainy and cold. He waited in line for half an hour for a taxi into Manhattan. Although the school district offered to put him up in a moderate accommodation, he chose a less expensive hotel in the theatre district on Eighth Avenue, off Times Square. The secretary at the Chancellor's office had been aghast when he told her where he was staying. She warned him to be careful. The neighborhood was sleazy, filled with prostitutes, drug dealers, and street people. After checking into his room, he walked through the neighborhood, absorbing the shops, bars, and theaters. The streets were full of people of all ethnicities, New York people the rest of the country found alien. No doubt about the energy. Nothing like where he lived. The atmosphere was exhilarating.

Next morning he packed his bag and waited for a call from the Chancellor. Nine o'clock, 10 o'clock, no call. He wondered if he should check out of his room.

At eleven the phone rang. It was Sam Kepner, the assistant.

"Something's come up," he said. "The Chancellor has an emergency at Bronx High School. He can't see you today. Can you stay over until tomorrow?"

"Yes, I guess so. You're paying for the room and flight change, I presume."

"Yes, yes, we'll take care of all that. Don't worry about it. We'll call you tomorrow. Enjoy New York in the meantime." He hung up.

That was abrupt, Reeder thought. First, they wanted him here immediately to talk about his report. Now they didn't. He doubted the story about the Chancellor. Maybe they were trying to decide how to handle him. He wondered how to spend the rest of his day. He pulled his address book from his briefcase and called Velma Williams.

"Hi, this is Paul Reeder," he said, as she answered. "I'm in town for a few days to see the Chancellor. Any chance of having a drink with me after work today?"

There was a long pause on the phone.

"I have a luncheon appointment. How about meeting me at the Museum of Modern Art at two? You said you liked artwork."

He met her at the museum. She was more conservatively dressed than before. A black suit, very business-like. He had worn his newest suit, a gray double-breasted with a nail-head pattern. The hang was perfect, he thought. They strolled through the museum, focusing on the most recent artwork. As they chatted, he could see she was knowledgeable about art. Many of the works made no sense to him, conceptual pieces by artists who had no ideas, but he was reluctant to appear ignorant. He let her do the talking. Occasionally, they brushed against one another as they walked through the galleries. He wondered if she was as aware of his presence as he was of hers.

He wasn't the only one critical of the artwork. As they passed a couple in the hallway, the man said, "The best piece of art that I have seen in this place is that man's suit," pointing at Reeder. The comment was aimed at the man's companion, who had probably dragged him to the exhibit.

Velma laughed. She was delighted.

"Oh, I am walking around with a classy artwork, am I?"

Reeder was flattered and embarrassed at the same time.

After forty-five minutes they came to an installation piece that people were crowding around. It was a mock-up of a cheap motel room with a man and a woman in bed, obviously after sex, the man well over on one side of the bed and the woman on the other. On the woman's side of the room were beautiful pieces of furniture, expensive lace and lingerie, lit candles, hearts and flowers, a bottle of champagne. On the man's side was the cheapest motel furniture, clothes strewn carelessly in haste, half a dozen empty beer cans lying on the floor. Apparently, the romantic partners saw the situation from different viewpoints, masculine, feminine, different worlds. The spectators were entranced. Reeder and Velma walked to the museum café without speaking, absorbed by the installation.

Reeder bought two cappuccinos and smiled at Velma as he sat them on the table.

"Makes you think, doesn't it?" Actually, he wondered what she was thinking.

"Yes, I guess that's what it's for. Disturbing, don't you think?"

"How do you mean?"

"Men and women, lovers, constrained to live in separate worlds, seeing their relationship so differently."

"Well, I do think women are inclined to see things more romantically than men, don't you?"

"That's what makes it so disturbing. You noticed none of the spectators were saying a thing."

"True, absorbing the impact, I guess."

"Like Frieda Kahlo. How different she was from Rivera. He could never have produced her work."

"Lacerated hearts?" Reeder had mixed feelings about Kahlo's work.

"Yes, something like that. I have seen lots of their work in Mexico. Hers is so personal. Emotional in a crude, distorted way."

"I thought you would like Rivera. More political."

"Oh, I do. Just the difference between male and female maybe. I admire his courage in not acceding to political pressure."

"You mean standing up to Rockefeller. Not changing his mural to make it acceptable. Even though Rockefeller destroyed it."

"I admire political courage."

"Well, maybe Rivera was just being self-indulgent."

They were reversing roles now. She was admiring those who took stands against political authority, which she represented, and he was contesting that. Gentle sparring. He enjoyed being with her. She was entertaining, intellectual, cosmopolitan.

"You seem very knowledgeable about art."

She smiled. "I come from what you call a privileged background. Good schools, lots of travel, all the right people." The last remark had a sardonic twist.

"I don't."

"I didn't think so."

"Maybe you could help me out by having dinner with me tonight. I keep dropping handfuls of mashed potatoes in my lap. Perhaps you could show me what I'm doing wrong."

"I have a better idea. Why don't I feed you? Say, my place at eight tonight."

Reeder felt drawn to her. The most attractive and clever woman he had met for a long time. But was this the proper way to relate to a client? The thought faded.

"Nothing would please me more."

CHAPTER TWENTY-SEVEN

It was a twenty-minute taxi ride to Velma's place in Greenwich Village. He didn't know how this dinner was going to play out. Her initiative had caught him off guard. Had she invited friends as well? He arrived about eight.

The brick apartment building was from the 1950s and not redone much over the years. Reeder paid the driver and rode the elevator to the fourth floor. Velma greeted him dressed in black top and pants. She was gorgeous. No doubt about it. And she was alone.

The apartment inside was like the outside, 1950s, with fixtures from that time. No one had made the effort to tear out the walls and open it up. It was small, a living room, a tiny kitchen, and a bedroom, but not bad for a New York apartment. The living room was larger than in newer buildings. The furnishings were cozy, overstuffed chairs, small wooden tables, floral and impressionist prints covering the walls. Some original artwork. More flowers. He would have guessed she would have contemporary furnishings and provocative art. The only modern touch was a computer near the window. She had been reading her e-mail. She invited him to sit in a stuffed chair and offered him a drink.

"What does the Chancellor want to see you about, by the way?"

"I don't think they were too happy about my first report. Especially the part about the test gains not being legitimate."

"Oh, yes. We noticed that in your report too. It contradicts their claims for the program's success, doesn't it?"

"Yes. My colleagues and I think so. Maybe the Chancellor wants to challenge me face to face. At least that's my guess." Reeder decided not to mention how angry the Chancellor was. He didn't know how much she knew. He would let her mention it.

"Will you change your mind about the test gains?"

"After I meet with him? Not likely. Unless he comes up with something we haven't thought of."

"Somehow that's what I thought you would say."

"Congratulations on the election, by the way. The Mayor really kicked ass."

"It helps when you run on both the Democratic and Republican tickets and have splinter candidates running against you. But it does give us a mandate for the next few years. Everyone in the office is really happy, including the Mayor. And the pressure is off."

"Big plans for the next year?"

"That's what I am working on now. Figuring out what we do next."

"I'll bet you are valuable to the Mayor. How did you get into politics?"

She ignored the compliment.

"I was involved in campus politics when I was in college. Radical undergraduate stuff, of course. That led to where I am now, via working on some political campaigns."

"You make it sound natural and easy."

"My father was a big campaign contributor. That opened some doors for me originally."

"Which party?"

"Any party that might help him. He was a hard-headed business man. Nothing ideological. But mostly to the Republicans, of course."

"Politics appeals to you, I gather. A sense of social justice maybe?"

"Maybe. I also like being around powerful people. People who make a difference. Motivations get confused sometimes, don't' they?"

He was surprised at her self-deprecating response. "Wow. That's a pretty honest self-assessment."

"Well, I paid for that insight. Ten years of analysis. True insights tend to be costly, don't you think? Just not as costly as not having them."

"In the social class I come from they skipped the insights and went straight for the behavior. Shock and cold wraps in the old days. Fire and ice. Pretty primitive stuff."

"It's mostly drugs now." She spoke as if she had special knowledge. He didn't pursue the issue.

She continued, "Maybe that's why I am attracted to you. A strong, powerful man."

"Me? Have you got the right guy? I don't see myself as powerful. All I do is comment on other people's actions."

She smiled. They talked an hour before she said the food was ready. She carried a steaming bowl of chicken and pasta from her kitchen to her dining table.

"A simple meal but I don't have much time when I work," she said.

"Looks great."

They finished the chicken and bottle of wine. Without asking, she opened another bottle. The conversation drifted from politics to the personal, how he liked New York, what it was like to live in the city.

After an hour she began clearing the table. He helped her carry dishes to the kitchen, brushing past her in the close space. The wine flushed his body and relaxed him. Nowhere else in the world existed, he felt. The drift of their conversation emboldened him and her revelations about herself made him feel as if he knew her better than he did.

He felt himself being drawn to her, this attractive, sophisticated woman. As she stacked dishes in the sink with her back to him, he leaned against her and put his arm around her waist. He put his nose in her hair. He could smell her perfume and feel the heat of her body through her clothes.

She became still. She turned around and looked into his eyes. He kissed her, and she did not back away. She was interested. He pushed against her, pressing her against the sink.

She pulled away and led him to her small bedroom, which was dark. She lit a candle on the table and closed the door so the candle provided the only light. He could see the shadows of the two of them on the wall. Plato's cave, he thought. As he looked around, he saw that she had stuck the candle in something white—a bowl of mashed potatoes! She was way ahead of him.

He couldn't help but laugh. Then he stopped laughing. Velma was removing all her clothing. Undressed, she was more voluptuous than she appeared in black. He lost interest in the shadows on the wall. He was drawn into her.

CHAPTER TWENTY-EIGHT

Next morning, his third day in town, the telephone in his hotel room rang. He was recovering from the night before. He had not gotten back to the hotel until early morning. It was Kepner, calling to tell him to come to the district administration building.

"We want you to come over to the Chancellor's office at ten. The Chancellor has an emergency and is too busy to see you, but George Clough, the Deputy, will see you. You met him before."

The hatchet man, Reeder thought. And from his appearance, an effective one. Reeder recalled the shadowy meeting during his first trip to town.

"Will you be there?" he asked.

"No, just you and the Deputy. The two of you."

That made it easier for the Deputy to deny what was said between them, if that became necessary. Reeder had no colleague with him. He had to play the cards he had been dealt.

"Ok, 10 o'clock. His office?"

"Yes." Kepner seemed less friendly. Something in his voice that wasn't there before. He gave no clue about the agenda. Reeder didn't ask. They had decided what to do with him.

It was a brisk, sunny day, though still cold. The traffic through town and onto the bridge was heavy. They drove over Brooklyn Bridge slowly and Reeder thought about Velma working in her office nearby. He arrived at 110 Livingston Street ten minutes early. He took the elevator to the top floor, pulling his flight bag behind him. The Deputy's secretary greeted him and seated him across from her desk. She didn't seem friendly either. Funny how assistants picked up vibes from their bosses.

The door to the Deputy's office was open, and Reeder could see in. The Deputy was sitting on a couch watching television. No one was in the office with him. Ten o'clock came and Reeder waited. Ten fifteen. The Deputy disappeared from view, presumably to go to his desk, which Reeder couldn't see from his chair. Finally, at 10.30 Deputy Clough rang the secretary to admit Reeder.

"You can go in now." She shut the door behind him.

The space was large, a corner office looking out over the city. It would make ten of Reeder's cubicle at the university. The Deputy was seated at an imposing oak desk facing the door. An American flag was on one side behind him and a New York flag on the other. Two couches formed an "L" near the television, which was turned off now. The furniture looked as if it had been around for a while, including the television set.

The Deputy rose from behind the desk, shook his hand without saying a word, and motioned Reeder to sit at the couch. He was half a head taller and leaner. He unbuttoned his coat. He didn't speak until he sat down on the other couch.

"I thought we hired you guys to help us, not hurt us." The Deputy was not smiling as he looked at Reeder.

"Well, we are trying to help you." It sounded feeble.

"Your report says that we don't have any test gains from the program. That doesn't help us. It makes us look bad." The report was not in sight anywhere. Clough knew what he wanted to say about it.

"True, but it saves you the embarrassment of someone from the outside finding out your testing office has not used the correct statistical analysis." Reeder cleared his throat.

"Look," the Deputy said, "You professors are a dime a dozen. I can hire professors to say anything I want them to say. Anytime I want. Right here in this city."

Reeder knew Clough was right. He could hire someone to say what he wanted. He was resorting to outright intimidation. Nothing disguised about it.

"Maybe so. But this regression analysis is not arbitrary. There is a right way and a wrong way to do it. You might hire someone to say what you want but sooner or later, someone outside New York, if not someone inside, will discover that the district has done the analysis wrong. And blow the whistle. Second Chance is a nationally known program. You'll be embarrassed. Better to face up to it and fix it now rather than later."

"That's your opinion. There are other experts around. And more than one way to do statistical analysis."

"Look, pretend that I'm a weapons expert, and I tell you that the bullets you are using in your gun are not the right caliber. And that sooner or later the gun is going to blow up in your hand if you continue to use that ammunition. I've have given you my best professional advice. If you want to take your chances anyhow, then go ahead. Fire away."

Reeder sat back on the couch, finished. The Deputy was silent for more than a full minute, which seemed to Reeder a long, long time. Neither man said anything, while Clough thought it over. Reeder had formulated the analogy, anticipating a negative reception. He thought the gun analogy was particularly appropriate for New York. He could hear horns honking and traffic on the streets below.

Finally, the Deputy said, "Well, ok. What if we do this? We put our analysis of the test scores into our report. Our analysis shows the gains. Then we add another page that shows the analysis based on the regression analysis. Your analysis, which shows no gains, on the next page. Readers would have both. Would that satisfy you?" His voice was softer, conciliatory.

"I think we can live with that," Reeder said right away, relieved the impasse had been broken. The tension between them drained away.

They spent fifteen minutes talking about details of Reeder's report. Reeder left the office wondering if Clough would turn the television back on. The confrontation had been over quicker than Reeder expected, though it had been intense. Head on. Sometimes encounters like these lasted days or weeks. He picked up his bag in the outer office, thanked the secretary, who said nothing, and caught a taxi to LaGuardia.

CHAPTER TWENTY-NINE

As the plane lifted off and headed for the Midwest, Reeder thought about the incident. He was elated that it had come off so well, in spite of the rough and tumble with the Deputy. He could live with the compromise they had reached about how to handle the regression effect in future evaluation reports. He had anticipated the confrontation might go on longer and involve more people, possibly resulting in cancellation of his monitoring role. He didn't want that right now. And not just because of professional reasons, he had to admit to himself.

As he put his head against the seatback, other thoughts crept into his mind . What had happened to the Chancellor, who had been so angry and insistent on seeing him? Reeder still had not met him. Did they figure the Deputy was better able to challenge Reeder head on? And why the delay in seeing him when they insisted he come immediately? Did they disagree about how to handle him? Were they arguing among themselves? He had no clue as to what went on behind the scenes the past few days. And he was unlikely to find out.

It was obvious that the Deputy kept him waiting outside the office deliberately. An attempt to put him in his place, to indicate to him that he was an obscure academic pitted against a large, powerful organization. Perhaps Reeder had been more resistant than they expected—though it had not taken the Deputy long to adjust the district position. It just seemed like a long time.

The compromise on the regression analysis must have been their fall-back position. What if Reeder had insisted that only the test scores showing no gains be presented? What would have happened? He didn't know. It was too late now. He couldn't go back on the agreement. That would be interpreted as bad faith on his part. But the agreement they reached was fair enough, he thought. It was the way such analyses were usually presented. He didn't regret not pushing the district further.

The flight attendants came down the aisle offering drinks. He bought a small bottle of red wine, which tasted harsh against his pallet. He looked at the label to see where it came from. Southern France. The airline was lowering costs again. Soon there would be no food at all. Maybe a good thing.

His thoughts turned to the night before with Velma. The night had been more than he bargained for. Their encounter had been more intimate than most of his sexual experiences. He felt himself open up to her and she to him. Why did he do that? Or was that his imagination? Not much had been said between them.

She was a gorgeous woman. And she was an unhappy woman too. He sensed sadness in her, though she had not revealed all that much about her past life. Maybe she had a lover. He didn't know. Nor had he said much about his personal life. What he was feeling after their night together was based on his intuitions, not on spoken words. One thing was clear. He wanted to see her again.

It was early evening by the time he got to his car at the airport. A light snow had fallen, dusting the car and the road. The snow was dry, powdery, no problem to drive in. A few flakes drifted down in the headlights of oncoming traffic. The back road through the cornfields, now barren, was safe to take as a shortcut.

He arrived at his house, exhausted after a long day, though he had met with the Deputy less than an hour. The tension fatigued him. And maybe the emotional contact with Velma. He opened a bottle of cabernet and listened to his phone messages. He could have retrieved them in New York but hadn't bothered. Messages from students about meeting with him, a message from a university committee announcing an emergency session, a message from his ex-wife, worried about their daughter. He would have to call her. A message from Penelope Reyes in New York wanting to meet with him. Damn! He had just been there.

He switched on his computer to check his e-mail, setting the wine glass on the desk so he didn't spill it on the computer. Junk messages and announcements from the university. He deleted them without bothering to read them. Three messages from colleagues. An e-mail from Sweden inviting him to give a speech at a conference in Stockholm in June. That could be interesting. He needed to get details before he decided whether to do it. He was too tired to respond tonight.

He switched to the financial Web sites. First, his university retirement funds invested in stocks and bonds. He checked the balances in his accounts to see how much they had changed in the past several days. Not much change. He switched to the website where he kept track of investments separate from his retirement funds. His Latin American fund had dropped two percent. It had been declining for two months. Maybe he should sell it.

Reeder was a more serious investor than his colleagues would have guessed. He started investing because the university retirement plan forced him to make investment choices. As with most things in life, he didn't like to make uninformed choices. He was too deliberate. At first he resented this intrusion on his life, at being forced to become an investor when he had no inclination. Then he became intrigued. Investing was a game. It had concrete rewards and punishments, immediate consequences, unlike academic life. Soon he began investing his consultant fees and book royalties.

His skills as an evaluator served him well. Attending to data, making unemotional decisions, and being careful about following popular trends paid off. Keeping his emotions under control was key. Most people were highly emotional about money. If he timed his actions right, he could make money by going against the crowd. The advice from most stockbrokers was to follow whatever investment fad was hot. They made money from commissions obtained by rolling over other people's investments. Too much conflict of interest to make their advice credible, even if they knew what they were talking about, which was doubtful. The pension funds advised ignoring market fluctuations altogether, investing over the long run and never taking money out until needed. That was good advice over thirty years. Who had that much time? As John Maynard Keynes had said, in the long run you're dead.

Reeder knew that he could not know what was going to happen in the markets before anyone else. A rube in the cornfields could hardly obtain information financiers on Wall Street had at their fingertips. It was preposterous to think that was possible. If he invested, he had to invest with knowledge of his own ignorance, knowing he could not have timely information. He knew that he didn't know. So he played the market averages the way he played black jack, calculating the odds and averages, just as you could not tell what card would be next in poker. You could make intelligent estimates.

He based his investments mostly on quantitative indicators, like the price-earnings ratio, running against the crowd when necessary, often buying when they sold and selling when they bought, keeping his eye on the data rather than on the euphoria of the latest market boom or the despair of a bust. When he guessed wrong, which was often, he cut his losses, most difficult to manage emotionally. And he had made several hundred thousand dollars.

As in poker, the trick was not simply to make money but not to lose it back. Right now, the stock market was high. It had been on an extended rally and appeared overvalued. The price-earnings ratio was heading into the stratosphere. He was nervous about stock prices plunging. So far he had done nothing other than watch the market closely. Perhaps he should begin switching money from stocks into safer investments. He went to bed and forgot about money. He thought about Velma, reliving their last night in his imagination.

CHAPTER THIRTY

At ten the next morning Reeder hurried to the administration building for a special session of the promotion committee. He could guess the reason for the urgency—the case of the archeologist who was accused of destroying Native artifacts. This meeting was not going to be pleasant.

Several committee members, including Vice-Chancellor Montclair were there when he arrived. The mood was somber and charged. Within a few minutes the VC closed the door, sat down, and started the meeting.

"As you remember, we have the case of Michael Skinner from archeology, who is accused of destroying artifacts while out on digs. Two of his colleagues sent photos of the destroyed artifacts. We voted last time to send the photos to Skinner and ask for his reaction. He has responded in a letter, copies of which I am passing out now, that he may have made a few mistakes on some field trips by drinking too much. However, he claims that his academic record is good enough to warrant promotion. He regrets whatever incidents may have occurred."

Jack Philips from English spoke first. "You mean he doesn't deny the allegations about the artifacts?"

"No, he doesn't deny them but he doesn't admit to them either. He leaves it ambiguous as to what he did. I guess since he doesn't deny the charges, it looks as if they could be true. In part at least. Or he may be following the advice of a lawyer."

Frank Ellis from psychology broke in. "I think we should promote him based on his academic record. That's what it says in the faculty handbook. Promotions should be based only on the candidate's record." Ellis had been thinking about the case apparently and thought he had found a way out.

Reeder disagreed. "Yes, but that presumes normal, civilized behavior. What he has done is an ethical violation. A serious one. I think we should vote against promotion for him. In fact, I would argue he should be dismissed from the university for such unethical conduct, if it is true."

Helen Moore from philosophy. "I agree. He should not hold a position at this university if he is capable of such behavior."

Montclair broke in. "This committee is organized to recommend promoting or not promoting faculty members. Not to decide whether they should be dismissed if they already hold tenured positions. Let's stick to the business at hand. Any decision on dismissal has to follow a different legal route. Our lawyers would have to be involved."

"I'm uncomfortable with denying him promotion based on ethical concerns. Research, teaching, and service are the criteria we have been given to base decisions on." Frank Eagleton from engineering.

"Well, don't you think that this is bad teaching, a bad role model for your students when you get drunk and destroy artifacts?" Moore said.

"I suppose you could look at it that way."

"I still think we should promote him based on his academic record. Publications, teaching, and service," Ellis said.

Reeder thought the committee was edging away from an important ethical issue. University faculty hated to make ethical judgments. They would rather say the archeologist was a bad teacher than say he was unethical.

"I still say the ethical issues are paramount. He violated an ethical trust."

"It doesn't say anything in the faculty handbook about destroying artifacts," Ellis said, raising his voice.

"No, and it doesn't say anything in the handbook about not torturing students either. There are certain actions we presume people will not do, that they will be ethical. You can't list every potential unethical act in the faculty handbook."

The argument was becoming heated. Ellis and Reeder had been at odds over ethics before, though not on an issue this dramatic. The Vice-Chancellor calmed the committee members down.

"Is there anyone here who has another opinion?"

George Harrington from biology had not said anything. "My opinion is that this is bad teaching and bad research. I don't have any hesitation in voting against promotion. Whether he should be dismissed from the university is another matter."

"Dismissal is not on the table for us to discuss, as I noted," Montclair said. He was brooking no discussion on this possibility.

The committee continued for an hour without anyone changing positions. They were wearing themselves out. The Vice-Chancellor sensed they had finished with the topic. Fatigue could end faculty discussions when nothing else could.

"Are we ready to vote? The issue is whether Professor Skinner should be recommended for promotion to full professor. How many are in favor?"

No one raised a hand. The VC looked at Ellis. "Frank?"

"I'm abstaining."

"Those opposed to promotion?"

The other faculty on the committee raised their hands.

"Promotion denied. We need to draft a letter to send to Skinner detailing why we have recommended against promotion. Of course, he has the right of appeal beyond this committee. And he remains an associate professor in the university, unless of course some other action is taken against him."

"Do you think some other action will be taken?" Moore asked.

"The legal department is looking into the possibilities. It's complicated, getting rid of a professor who is tenured. It is not done often, as you know. But it is done sometimes."

"Like when?" Reeder was skeptical that the university would do anything so decisive.

"The most recent case I can remember was a faculty member falsifying grades for football players. That was about four years ago. We got rid of him when we found out about it. I won't reveal the name of the department. It's a department that enrolls many of our athletes."

Reeder didn't remember the case. The university had hushed it up. Administrators didn't like bad publicity for the university, preferring instead to make large cash settlements and include the silence of the participants as a binding part of the legal agreement.

The VC thanked the committee for a difficult job accomplished and dismissed them.

"I don't need to remind you how delicate this case is. Talking about it outside this room can cause mischief. Serious mischief. I am sure you understand that. Professor Reeder, can I talk to you for a moment?"

As the other committee members filed out the door, Reeder walked to the head of the table to hear what Montclair had to say.

"Paul, I understand where you are coming from about the ethical issue but this is a complicated case. We have to get the lawyers involved. Otherwise, we'll get out butts sued off."

"I understand that. It's just that we can't let the lawyers decide everything and throw ethics out the window. We have to take a stand on these things."

"I agree fully, and I appreciate your speaking out in the meeting. It's not easy to take ethical stands these days."

As Reeder left the administration building, he thought it was interesting that the VC had taken him aside to clarify his position. Maybe conscience and principle weren't gone in the university entirely, even among administrators. Then again, maybe the VC was agreeing with all sides, even when they contradicted each other. That had been done often enough.

CHAPTER THIRTY-ONE

A few weeks later the next evaluation report on the Second Chance retention program arrived from New York. Reeder examined it closely to see how they handled the regression analysis. He was not surprised to see that they made the program appear more positive than he would have. But then the evaluation office was part of the school district.

He didn't know for certain but he suspected the evaluation reports were not allowed to leave the central administration until they had been scrutinized by the Chancellor's office. The Deputy had demonstrated detailed knowledge about the program and the evaluation, as if he had read the previous evaluation reports carefully and perhaps participated in their composition. Administrative oversight was common in large bureaucracies. Top administrators could not depend on their technical experts to display enough public relations sensitivity.

At the very end of the text, on page 56 of the report, was the presentation of the test score data, showing test gains, and on page 57 the corrected test scores taking regression to the mean into consideration, showing no test score gain. Reeder was disappointed there was no detailed explanation of the two different sets of scores in the text.

He should have insisted on textual explanation but he had not, he remembered. An oversight on his part, not serious, but he should have thought of it. Overall, the report was what he agreed to in his compromise with the Deputy. He had no complaints. He would address his concerns about the lack of explanation in response to this district report. One thing at a time. He was making progress with them.

After reading the report he put it on his desk, which was cluttered with work he had neglected over the past several weeks. The New York project was preoccupying him, not to mention his relationship with Velma. He could not get her out of his mind. He found that disturbing. After all, he didn't know her that well.

He glanced out the window at the accumulating snow settling over the prairies and turned to a journal article he had been working on for two months. The topic was the politics of evaluation in complex organizations. He had promised the piece for a special issue of a journal. The article was far from finished. In fact, he had lost his train of thought. He started rereading what he had written. He didn't like what he had done. Maybe he should not have agreed to write the article. Maybe he didn't have that much to say.

His phone rang.

"Hello, Professor Reeder? This is Elaine Katzanis from the New York comptroller's office. You don't know me but I am assigned to keep track of the school district's retention program, the Second Chance program, for my office."

Reeder knew about the comptroller's office. Velma Williams had briefed him. Ordinarily, comptroller offices kept track of budgets to ensure that funds were not misspent. But the New York office was more powerful. When the city went bankrupt, the reorganization of city finances put the comptroller's office in charge of the city budget. The comptroller's office could approve projects from a substantive as well as from a financial perspective. It had the authority to shut off funds to city agencies. The office had been successful in helping the city resurrect its financial solvency. At a price. Other city agencies feared the comptroller's intervention with good reason.

Traditionally the comptroller's office was used as a springboard into city politics, and the current comptroller was a man with strong political ambitions. It was said he would like to be Mayor. Although he was of the same political party as Mayor Kuhnsmiller, there was no love lost between them. They saw each other as competitors, not colleagues. Velma had briefed Reeder on the comptroller's ambitions and the power he exercised through the budget. Reeder needed to be cautious.

"What can I do for you, Ms. Katzanis?"

"I have been reading the latest evaluation report on the Second Chance program and I am puzzled. It says in the district report that there are test gains resulting from the program. But the Mayor's office tells me you say those gains are nullified by something called a regression effect. I don't see that in this report. Is that true?"

"Well, I have agreed to report only to the Mayor's office and the Chancellor's office in confidence. But I think you will find information on the regression effect in the district evaluation report."

"The Chancellor's office is not very forthcoming in revealing what they are up to. They conceal things. I can't get anything out of them on this topic. I think they are giving me the runaround."

He picked up the district evaluation report and found the table.

"You'll find the corrected test scores on page 57 in their report. Do you have it handy?"

"Yes, I have it in my hand right now. Which page again?"

"The table on page 57."

There was a long pause as Reeder heard her turning pages.

"Which page?"

"Page 57."

Another pause.

"I don't have a page 57. The copy I have ends on page 56, which shows the test score gains."

They had sent her a copy with page 57 and the regression corrections missing. Reeder didn't know what to say.

"I am afraid they have sent you a copy of the report with the regression analysis missing." He repeated the obvious.

"Those son-of-a-bitches! Those dirty son-of-a-bitches!"

She lost the official tone of her voice.

"Those bastards! They have deliberately sent me a copy with the test score analysis missing! I told you that you can't trust them any farther than you can throw them!"

Reeder still didn't know what to say. The omission looked deliberate.

"Why don't you call them and suggest that they have sent you a defective copy and that you need another one. If they won't send you one, I will send you a copy of mine."

She was furious.

"Never mind! I'll take care of those bastards!"

She slammed the receiver down without saying goodbye.

Reeder sat stunned for a moment. Then he laughed aloud, throwing his head back. What audacity! You had to admire them for their chutzpah. Unquestionably a New York quality, in case he ever doubted it.

CHAPTER THIRTY-TWO

The clouds were dark and hanging low in the sky when Reeder arrived at Neil's house. Looked like snow clouds. Neil's place sat modestly among the other little white frame houses. Neil was the only academic who lived in the working class neighborhood, other than a few assistant professors biding their time until they earned enough to move to a better part of town.

Neil's house was well cared for, better than the others. No doubt because of Roy. Neil hired a part-time handy man to look after the place, including the inside, the outside, and whatever piece of junk Neil was driving at the time. In fact, Neil relied on Roy to find him cars, always very cheap and very used. It took Roy's skills to keep them running.

Neil was looking for Reeder out the window and answered the door before he could knock. The ubiquitous whiskey glass was in his hand. As usual the little house was filled with cigarette smoke.

"Glad to see you. I haven't seen you in weeks."

"I have been out of town a lot, and busy in general. That time of year. Your house looks nice. Have you painted it recently?"

"Oh, yes, Roy did that. He said it needed it, which I guess it did. I never notice. Of course, my daughter has been after me about Roy."

"For what?"

"She says I take advantage of him. Exploit him. The middle-class professor taking advantage of a working class bloke. The way he takes care of me."

"Well, that's an extreme interpretation, isn't it?"

"You damned right. Ever since she got her psychoanalysis degree from the institute, she has been psychoanalyzing me too. Damned uncomfortable! Sometimes she's more accurate than I like!"

"You need someone to look after you, don't you? I doubt you could manage on your own." Neil's helplessness in everyday matters was legendary, though some of it was pretense. People felt sorry for him and did things for him that way. It was unclear how much was real and how much fabricated to gain favors. He probably didn't know himself.

"Hey, don't you start too! I think Sharon wants me to live with her and her family. I am not about to do that." Neil poured a glass of whiskey and handed it to Reeder without asking if he wanted one. Nothing had changed inside. The place looked the same. No new paintings. Neil's amateur painter must be on sabbatical.

"Where is Roy? I haven't seen him around."

"He was here yesterday, cleaning up the garden. Besides, as I tell her, Roy needs the money. He has three kids and barely gets by as it is."

"Seems like a reasonable trade-off to me."

Neil switched the topic.

"Where have you been recently? New York?"

"Yes, the New York project with the school district and the Mayor's office."

Reeder told him how the statistical analysis showing no test score gains had played out, how he had written this conclusion into the monitoring report, and had sent copies to the Mayor and Chancellor's offices.

"Yes, yes! What happened then?" Neil was sitting on the edge of his seat so excited he was forgetting to smoke his cigarette, the ash of which fell on the floor. Neil enjoyed the story so much that Reeder regretted not coming around more often to keep him informed. The trade was still in his blood, especially the politics, which he thrived on.

Reeder told him about the meeting with the Deputy.

"Ha, ha, he was trying to intimidate you! No doubt about it!"

Reeder built to the climax, the phone call from the comptroller's office about the report with the missing page. Reeder was enjoying telling the story as much as Neil was hearing it.

Neil threw back his head and laughed about the missing page.

"No shit! No shit! Well, I'll be damned. I have seen a lot of things but that's a new one on me."

"Yeah, wild, isn't it?" Reeder went on,"I guess the question for me now is what I do about it. Do I call them and protest or what?" Reeder took a sip of whiskey.

Neil put out his cigarette and lit another one while he thought for a minute. The butt in the ashtray simmered.

"Well, if it were me, I think I would let it go. Not mention it to the school district administrators."

"Why would you do that?"

"First of all, there is nothing you can prove. They can say they simply made a mistake on her copy. And if there are other copies like that sent to other people, they can say there were several bad copies of the report with the missing page. Clerical error."

"Maybe it really was a mistake."

"No, no, it wasn't a mistake. Of course not. They did it deliberately. And chances are they might have gotten away with it, except the woman in the comptroller's office is on their trail. You wouldn't have known the difference if she hadn't called you."

"Yes, that is true."

"They can just say it was a mistake. The second thing is that the comptroller's office knows now and if they are as powerful as you say they are well able to take care of the matter, better than you can. The district won't do that again!"

"That's what I am told anyhow." He noticed that Neil was lighting another cigarette. He had two smoking in the ashtray now and one in his mouth.

"Third, the Chancellor's office will know you know because the woman will tell them. By not mentioning it to them, you will appear to them that you know more than you are saying to them. Which gives you an advantage. They don't know what you do know because you don't tell them everything you know. You could be saving stuff up for future use, as far as they are concerned. They have to be cautious in dealing with you."

"Christ, you are getting too devious for me now! This is beginning to sound like one of these convoluted contrivances of yours that backfires!"

Neil had a devious mind. If there were two ways to do something, a straightforward way and a devious way, he always chose the devious path. This tactic often backfired on him because people became suspicious of his deviousness. He never accepted the fact that the straightforward way could be the most effective. Reeder's own inclination was to be as direct as possible if he could.

"No, no, you don't have to worry about that! You are not concocting a plot! You are just not telling them that you know. By not saying anything, it might lead them to trust you with more things that they wouldn't trust you with otherwise."

"Shit! You're devious!"

Neil finished off his glass of whiskey and lit another cigarette at the same time. Neil did have brilliant insights into human nature. And he also had incredibly bad ones, as his career and life demonstrated. The problem for Reeder was to tell the brilliant insights from the terrible ones. It wasn't easy.

Reeder was thinking about his next trip to New York to talk to people he had not contacted. He needed to make a trip to collect information from those who had asked to talk to him, particularly Penelope Reyes and the parent union. And there was no denying that Velma Williams was part of his thinking as well. He had more than professional reasons to visit New York as soon as he could.

CHAPTER THIRTY-THREE

Ten days later Reeder met Penelope Reyes in New York at a delicatessen on Sixth Avenue near Central Park. She had chosen their meeting place. He didn't know why. Perhaps it was midway between her school and his hotel. It had been years since he had seen her, and when she walked in he was struck that she looked older and heavier. He probably did too. She was five years older then he. He waved to her from his table.

"Penelope," He said, as he rose to greet her. "How are you?"

"Good. How about yourself?"

"Fine. I see your name all over the newspapers. You have hit the big time."

"The media wear me out. But I guess it's part of the job."

"Well, a deserved celebrity in any case. You have done what most of us only talk about."

Reyes was well known nationally, and especially in New York, for the school she had established for students from poor backgrounds. Most of her students were from minority groups, and they went on to achieve far beyond normal expectations. Ninety percent went to a university and most graduated. An astounding record, considering their backgrounds.

"How many years has it been since I last saw you? Five?

"Something like that."

He couldn't remember the last time. They had met years before when he was doing evaluations of alternative schools. Unlike most reforms, her ideas stressed democratic principles for students and staff.

"Well, you certainly have come a long way since then. You are a real voice for democratic schooling."

"I hope so. For the right kind anyhow. I hope we counter some of the airhead ideas about letting kids go off on their own without guidance. They need structure like anyone else. And they need it from adults."

"I wouldn't think the lack of structure was such a big problem these days. Not in schools anyhow. Considering all the back-to-basic reforms politicians are pushing through."

The waiter brought a menu and they ordered salads.

"I agree. Including the city's Second Chance program."

"Yes, including that one."

"That's what I wanted to talk to you about. I hear that you are the overseer for the evaluation of Second Chance."

"Yes, that's true. I am not doing the evaluation, you understand. I am just monitoring the district's evaluation. A kind of audit. Where did you hear about that?"

"I have my sources. From people I know and the staff of the parent union. They don't like the program. I keep informed, though my school is not part of it, of course."

Reyes had not only succeeded in her school, but she had done it within the New York school system, a remarkable achievement, considering how rigid the system was. Years before she had talked administrators into letting her start a school that didn't have to follow the mandates of the district. A political feat in itself. She knew district politics, though she was never able to persuade the central office to establish other schools like hers. However, other schools around the country followed her lead. She was so prominent that the district could not rescind the freedom they had given her, even if they regretted it.

"What's your take on Second Chance?"

"Well, you won't be surprised to know I think it is wrong-headed. Actually detrimental to kids to flunk and be held back in school. It almost guarantees they will drop out when they are old enough."

"I am not surprised at your opinion. Of course, my job is to oversee the evaluation, not persuade the district that their policies are wrong, even if I thought that. I have a circumscribed role."

"Yes, I know that. Or at least I heard that. That's what I wanted to talk to you about. I hear some schools involved in the program are cheating on the tests they give to students. So the test score gains are inflated in some cases."

"You think there is large-scale cheating going on?" He wasn't surprised there might be some cheating, but how much was there?

"Yes, that's what I hear. Many principals and teachers feel they have their backs against the wall. The district is threatening to replace them or shut down their schools if they don't raise test scores. And, of course, some are concerned about what will happen to the kids being flunked."

"So they help matters along by falsifying the test results?"

"Hell, people will cheat on their eye exams if they have to. Educators are like anyone else."

Reeder laughed. "I see you haven't lost your old socialist beliefs about human nature."

Like many New Yorkers of her generation she had been a socialist in her younger days. Her school reform centered on decision making by the faculty and students. On the other hand, she was not afraid to boot someone out who didn't fit in with her plans. She governed with a firm hand. Also a left-wing trait.

"Those beliefs have served me well, even if we don't have a socialist movement worthy of the name anymore. Whatever happened to the left wing in this country?" From time to time she contributed articles to political journals.

"Do you have proof of the cheating?"

"No, I don't have proof. But I believe it's happening. I thought I had better tell you. It could affect the results of the evaluation, couldn't it?"

"Yes, it could, it definitely could, if it is widespread enough."

"That's why I thought I should tell you."

"Where did you hear about it again?"

"As I say, I have my sources and they are pretty good. I'll leave it at that."

"I appreciate you letting me know. It could be important. Do you know if the cheating comes from the central office or from individual schools?"

"Don't know. Individual schools, I think. I haven't heard anything about the central office being involved. I wouldn't put it past them though."

Reeder laughed again. Her disdain for the administrative hierarchy had not diminished. It was good to see someone who had succeeded so dramatically without being compromised in the process. In exchange for her information, Reeder told her about the missing page in the report sent to the Comptroller's office. She laughed so hard she had to stop eating and take a drink of water.

As they finished lunch they switched to national politics. Penelope was a pleasure to talk to, her integrity as intact as ever. He hoped he could manage his own half as well.

CHAPTER THIRTY-FOUR

Next morning Reeder crossed Brooklyn Bridge and arrived at 110 Livingston Street at 10 o'clock. The evaluation office was on the sixth floor. It was cramped, with desks, filing cabinets, and people crammed into every corner. He couldn't see how many rooms there were but not enough. Of course, evaluation and testing offices looked like this. There was never enough space to keep all the proliferating data.

Rick Cole, the Director of Evaluation and Testing, came out of his office to greet Reeder. He was cordial, even friendly, in spite of Reeder's criticism of the handling of the test score analysis. Perhaps Cole was trying hard. In any case, no ill feelings were apparent.

"You want to see test results for individual schools?"

"Yes, if you don't mind. As I indicated over the phone, I would like to check out how different schools have improved their test results year by year."

"Sure, no problem. Of course, we have a lot of schools. Hundreds. I'll set you up in a supply room and give you some printouts to look at. Do you want me to go over the data with you?"

"No, that's not necessary. If I have some questions, I'll come ask."

Cole led him to a side room stacked with paper. On the table in the crowded room were stacks of computer printouts. Pounds and pounds of them. Reeder took off his suit jacket, rolled up his sleeves, and sat down at the table, steeling himself for a long day. He began looking at the test data school by school.

As he glanced down the columns of numbers, he could see differences in test results year by year. Some schools had little change in their average test scores from one year to the next, some schools' test scores went down, and some schools showed large increases. Reeder noted the increases that averaged more than fifteen percent over the past year. That would be quite large for a school in one year. He wrote the names of the schools on a pad of paper and underlined those with average test gains over twenty percent.

He worked all day, sipping coffee and refusing lunch when Cole came to see if he was hungry. It was too bad he didn't have scores for individual items on the tests. From those he could see whether scores on particular items had increased dramatically. That might indicate whether teachers were teaching particular test items, such as spelling words from the test. However, the commercial test maker did not provide individual item results for each school. The district would be even more inundated with data if the publisher had.

He did have subtest scores to look at so he could see whether there were gains for reading passages versus language usage and vocabulary. The Cosmopolitan Reading Test consisted of six subtests. Some subtests were easier to teach to than others. Teaching students test items dealing with comma use or the spelling of words was easier than teaching them how to read and interpret passages, a generic skill. He examined subtest scores for schools with the greatest increases. The data confirmed his suspicions.

By 3 o'clock his neck was stiff and his eyes were blurry. He had had nothing to eat. He took his list of schools into Cole's office. Cole was sitting at his desk typing into his machine. He looked up.

"Finished?"

"Yeah, I think so, for today anyhow."

He sat down in a chair while Cole asked his secretary to bring them one more acrid cup of coffee.

"I have been looking at individual schools that have the highest test score increases. Do you have a map indicating where these schools are located in the city?"

"Sure. Right there." Cole pointed to a large map on his wall. "I need the map to find the damn schools when I have to visit them. I don't have a clue to the location of many of them, even after six years in this job."

Together they located the schools on the map. Reeder read out the names of the ones with the highest test score increases while Cole found them and marked their location with green thumbtacks. After plotting twenty of the highest scores, they stopped to inspect their work.

The schools were not located randomly across the city. Most of the schools were concentrated in two areas. Others were scattered.

"What are those two areas where those schools are concentrated?"

"I think they are concentrated in two subdistricts, this one in Manhattan and this one in the Bronx." Cole traced the faint green lines on the map with his finger.

"The New York City school district is divided into twenty-four subdistricts, each headed by a superintendent who reports to the Chancellor. This structure resulted from decentralizing the administration of the schools years ago. We have had mixed results from it, in my opinion. Of course, we never say that publicly."

"Who's in charge in those subdistricts?"

Cole fumbled around in his desk until he found the district organization chart.

"Andrew Brown in Manhattan and Bernie Schwartz in the Bronx. Both have been around for some time. They both came up through the ranks. Very different personalities though. Brown is pretty casual, a sharp dresser. Schwartz is very ambitious, would like to be Chancellor some day. I know them because they are both focused on the scores."

"Do you think I could visit a few schools we have identified?"

"Sure, no problem. What are you looking for?"

"I am interested in how the schools with the largest test score increases have managed to achieve such impressive gains."

Reeder was not ready to share his suspicions yet. What he said was true. He was interested in how the schools achieved their gains. What he suspected was that some schools had done it by manipulating student scores. How did they do it, if they had?

CHAPTER THIRTY-FIVE

As the taxi pulled up in front of Claire Barton Elementary School, Reeder thought, yes, this is what they are like. Ugly. It was a three-story turn of the century school building, gray and grim. He wondered if the students attending the school when it was brand new had had the same impression. Probably not. They would have been new immigrants from Europe anxious to make it in the New World, grateful to attend a school, any school. Their parents would harp about how important it was to learn English, perhaps refuse to allow them to speak their native language at home. And the immigrants had made it, for the most part. The schools had delivered.

Since then something had gone wrong. Now the schools were disdained, reviled, and blamed for society's many ills. Yet the public schools were much the same as when Reeder attended them. If anything they were better. Something had changed in the perception of the schools more than in the schools themselves. Or in what was expected of them. Reeder himself was one more plague inflicted on them, he thought, as he walked up the front steps.

The principal was expecting him. He was standing at the door to let him in. He was a nervous, short little man with a balding head. Who wouldn't be nervous if the central office called to say a visitor was coming with an unknown mission? Principal Hoffman led Reeder to his office, not bothering to introduce him to the secretaries at the desks.

"You want to visit some classrooms?"

"I would prefer to talk to some teachers who are teaching in the Second Chance program."

"Yes, yes, Mrs. Chin has a free period right now. I will see if she is in the teacher's lounge." The principal left to get her.

The test results for this school looked too good to be true. The students in the school showed large gains over the past year. Standardized achievement test scores were not that easy to improve. They were constructed to be stable measures of knowledge. Easy items most students would get right were tossed out. So were difficult items few students would get right. The tests were not based on the material being taught in the classroom. This made them insensitive to student learning.

There were several ways to cheat on the tests. One way was to teach the students the answers to the tests directly. If you taught that Shakespeare wrote Hamlet and that was the exact item on the test, getting it right did not indicate students had much knowledge of Shakespeare. In addition to the test items, you could teach material close to what was on the test. You could teach comma usage for two weeks before the test was given if you knew commas were emphasized. If each student got only one or two extra items correct, it made a huge difference in the percentile scores. Or you could take student answer sheets and doctor them up by changing answers. Or you could manipulate which students took the test. All Reeder could do was get an idea of what was going on. He couldn't monitor hundreds of schools.

Mrs. Chin came in. She was a young woman in her early 20s, very thin, with a sweater wrapped around her, in spite of how hot it was in the building. She had not been teaching long. Reeder talked to her about her Second Chance class. She was enthusiastic. After five minutes he edged toward the topic of the tests.

"What about when they give the citywide reading test. Do you do any special preparation for that?"

Mrs. Chin thought for a moment. "No, not really, just the usual preparation materials from the subdistrict curriculum office."

"What are those materials like? Could I see some of them?"

She left and returned in a few minutes with a bundle of materials. She handed them to him.

"I have class in ten minutes," she said, wrapping her sweater around her more tightly.

"Oh, right. Sorry I am taking up your time."

She was puzzled about what he was looking for but she didn't ask.

He looked through the materials she had given him. From what he could tell, the materials were based closely on the Cosmopolitan Reading Test. The format was not only the same as the test format but he suspected some vocabulary words were identical. He wasn't sure. It was not unusual for school districts to prepare students for the tests. The question was how close the materials were to the test.

Mrs. Chin was unaware there might be anything wrong with teaching materials the subdistrict office sent her. She probably had never seen the

Cosmopolitan Test. They sent her the material and she taught it diligently, apparently very diligently from the test results for the school. The test had different forms that were administered in different years, in order to prevent access to test items. But there were only a few forms. And over the years it was no problem to secure copies of all the forms. For that matter the Cosmopolitan was not a secure test. Anyone who was persistent could obtain copies.

Reeder thanked her and talked to two more teachers during their coffee breaks. The results were the same. Materials from the subdistrict office arrived six weeks before the test was given. The teachers were asked to use the preparation materials. They did so to varying degrees. No one came around to check on them to see if they did. But the test gains for the students in the Second Chance program had been dramatic. To be certain he needed to check the actual test items against the materials.

He doubted the principal knew much about it. The materials came from the subdistrict curriculum office. Of course, he could be wrong about that. Reeder sketched his next moves as his mind raced through the possibilities and the way to track them.

CHAPTER THIRTY-SIX

He met Velma at a French restaurant in the Village, a small one with only four tables, a favorite place of hers. The owner chef prepared the food in a tiny kitchen a few feet away while his wife served the tables. Velma was waiting for him there when he arrived. He had forgotten how gorgeous she looked.

They sat at a small table in the front corner near the window.

"How did your visit go?" she asked.

"Good. The district is being very cooperative at the moment. By the way, did you get a call from a woman in the comptroller's office a few weeks back?"

"Oh, yes," she said. "And she called me back after she found out the last page in the evaluation report was missing. She was furious! Can you imagine them sending her a copy without the last page?"

"No, I guess I am a little naive when it comes to New York politics. Just a simple guy from the Midwest."

She laughed. "Well, this trick threw me too, if that is any consolation. I haven't encountered this before. I hear she really reamed out the Chancellor's office good. Of course, they declared it was an innocent mistake. She didn't believe them for a instant."

"I may have some more bad news for them. I am afraid some of the schools may be cheating on the citywide test. I am not certain but it seems likely."

He should not have told her what he was working on since she was involved with the program. He was blurring the personal and professional with her. More than a little.

"Really? Would they do that?"

"They might. People think of teachers as being professional and ethical, which they are, but when their backs are against the wall, they behave like anyone else."

"That's interesting. I wonder how they do it, the cheating?"

"That's what I am looking into."

He remembered the archeologist at his university who was destroying artifacts. It was too good a story not to impress her with. He should not have told her that either. They ordered food and a bottle of white wine. The talk drifted to personal matters.

"Do you live alone?" she asked.

"Yes, after my wife left me, I have lived by myself." He thought he would get it out in the open that his wife left him, not the other way around. He didn't want to deceive Velma. She didn't ask why.

"I find I prefer living by myself. Starts to worry you after a while, how much you like being alone."

"I know what you mean. But you don't want to be alone all the time."

"No, it does leave out a few things."

"I've lived by myself since I was divorced. A long time now."

Since she mentioned it, he thought he would pursue the topic.

"How long were you married?"

She didn't answer directly but drifted off, caught by another idea.

"When I was a child, we had lots of woods on our property, and I played by myself in the woods all alone. Until my sister was older."

He didn't say anything, waiting for her to continue.

"Fourteen months. That's how long I was married. I was in Florence, spending a few months there, studying art. And I met him there."

"An Italian?"

"No, he was an American. Same background as me. Northeast, Ivy League. His family was in finance. We came back to the States together. My father didn't like him. Which probably made him more appealing. My father didn't approve of many things I did."

"What happened?"

"We found out we didn't really know the person each of us married."

"That's not unusual."

"No, true. Neither is divorce."

"I guess you have to wonder how much people really know who they are married to."

She didn't respond. After her confession, he felt obliged to reveal something about himself. He told her how he had wandered into the evaluation field, an unplanned career that he had stuck with. And that it suited his overly critical temperament. She laughed at his confession.

"I do know that evaluation and marriage don't mix. Not inside the same time and place anyhow," he volunteered. But she didn't pursue the hint.

The meal came and it was superb, as she said it would be. By the time they finished a heavy snow was falling. They walked into the street.

"Do you want to come back to my place?" she asked.

"Sounds like a great idea!"

They walked to the main street to flag a taxi. The snowfall was heavy, and there were no taxis in sight. Fifty feet down the street an African American woman was trying to flag down a taxi unsuccessfully. She was covered with snow, as if she had been standing on the corner for a while. She must have been working at one of the local businesses as a cleaning lady.

Finally, a taxi drove down the street and the woman waved at it. The taxi driver ignored her and drove past her to stop where Reeder and Velma were standing. Without hesitation Velma opened the door and jumped in out of the snow. Reeder followed reluctantly, glancing at the woman who was watching them take the taxi. Reeder felt bad about it but hesitated to say anything to Velma.

Soon they were back at her place. She unlocked the door and walked in.

"Coffee? A drink?"

"No, I don't think so." He was still buzzed from the wine.

"Me either. You are what I want. No reservations."

As she dropped her coat on the couch she turned to him and pressed herself against him, kissing him on the mouth. She turned and went directly to the bedroom where she lit a candle and began undressing. He followed, his head full of feelings about her.

CHAPTER THIRTY-SEVEN

Next morning Reeder called Rick Cole at the evaluation office and said he wanted to talk to him. Cole told him to come straight over. When Reeder walked into the office, Cole had a man and a woman with him. Witnesses. Whatever else Cole was, he wasn't stupid. Reeder recognized the man as one who had been at the mysterious evening meeting the first trip to New York. Cole introduced the man and woman as his assistants.

"What can we do for you?"

"I think we may have a problem."

"I figured that since you spent so much time here in the office the other day."

"Looking at the test data from the Second Chance program, it looks to me as if there might be some fudging of test scores going on."

Cole didn't bat an eye, nor did his colleagues. Maybe this was not news to them. They waited for Reeder to continue, revealing nothing.

"I visited a couple of schools yesterday and found out the subdistricts are supplying teaching materials to the teachers that are pretty close to the tests."

"It's not unusual to prepare students for the tests. All school districts do it."

"No, it's not unusual. But I don't think that's what this test preparation is. It's more than that. Maybe. And the scores themselves seem to confirm that. Some of those gains are hard to believe."

"Maybe."

Cole was not surprised, Reeder could see. Cole must have known what Reeder was up to when he inspected the test data. And helped him along without providing any clues other than what he was asked. A cool customer. Maybe that's what it took to work your way up in a massive bureaucracy and survive.

"What do you want us to do about it?" Cole said. He was challenging Reeder to make the case explicit.

"I want you to check to see if that is the case, if there is systematic cheating going on. It could make a difference in the test results."

"What do you want specifically?"

"Conduct a special study of the test scores of the students in those two subdistricts to see how inflated the scores are in specific schools."

"You mean from the past test data you looked at the other day."

"Right. I want to see how widespread the problem is and to quantify it as best we can."

"What else?"

"Second, examine the materials being used for test preparation in these two subdistricts and in all the other subdistricts."

Cole's unnamed assistants were taking notes but not saying anything.

"Anything else?"

"Interview some teachers in these schools to see what the practice of teaching these materials has been and trace the source of the materials that are used. Find out who provided them and ordered them used. In the meantime the test results from these two local districts in particular should be regarded with suspicion."

"Anything else?"

"That about covers it for the time being."

"You are asking for a lot. I need you to put these requests in writing before I act on them. In one of your official monitoring reports. The Chancellor and Mayor have a lot riding on this program. If I do what you want on my own, I could be full of more holes than the old punch cards we used with the mainframes."

So Cole knew what was going on. And he let Reeder figure it out for himself. Now he wanted authorization and cover to proceed to disclose the cheating. No, he wasn't stupid. He had been around the bureaucracy a long time.

"Ok, I'll put it in writing."

"You'll need to reveal your suspicions explicitly."

"About the possible cheating?"

"Yes, about the possible cheating."

"Agreed. I will have to check with my colleagues back on campus, but it should be no problem. I'll give you a call when I get back there."

Reeder knew that if the cheating accusation didn't prove out, it would be on his head, not Cole's. And it would look especially bad coming so soon after the criticism about the regression effect. As he left the office Reeder sensed that Cole was feeling better about the situation than he was. Perhaps it was just his imagination.

CHAPTER THIRTY-EIGHT

The flight back was routine, except for an ugly incident on the plane. The plane was full, and Reeder was upgraded to business class between New York and Chicago, a payoff for the miles he flew every year. Before the plane took off, a burly businessman across the aisle started wolfing down free drinks. He had four double vodka martinis before the flight attendants served food. Reeder could see the flight attendants were concerned about the man's drinking and tried to cut him off, but the fat man insisted when they delayed serving him.

An hour into the flight, the man fell asleep. The flight attendants served a meal, steak with salad, while the man snored. The passengers ate their meals in silence when suddenly the snoring man chortled, gagged, and spit a gob of phlegm straight into the salad of the man sitting next to him. The fat man settled back into his chair still asleep. Reeder could see the gob glistening on the green salad across the aisle.

The man with the salad was furious. He said something to his seat partner on the other side, who also had noticed the spitting. The offended man tried to awaken the drunk, shaking him, but couldn't arouse him. The drunk was dead to the world. An hour later the plane landed in Chicago and the drunk awoke. The offended man, still indignant, told the drunk what he had done. For a moment Reeder thought there was going to be a fight as they left the aircraft, but the fat man apologized, looking chagrined.

Reeder arrived home long after dark. The weather was turning colder. Mail filled his mailbox, but it was junk and bills. He tossed most of it into the garbage without opening it. He checked the messages on his work phone and found two from students and a reminder of a committee meeting.

He thought about the incident on the plane. He could see why the man whose salad it was had been so offended. It was a breach of personal space, someone assaulting his identity. Thinking about it, Reeder wondered if the offended man came from the working class. The way he clenched his fist and nearly hit the drunk made Reeder think he must be. Transgression, aggressors invading your space. When you were adult, you didn't have to take that anymore.

Reeder imagined how the man must have felt when the drunk spit in his salad. Reeder felt rage against the drunk even now. Sometimes old feelings surged back. An incident, a comment, a gesture might bring suppressed rage spewing from below. He was not sure he would have restrained himself as well.

Here he was a scholar with scores of publications, and he was thinking about slugging a man on an airplane because the man spit in someone's salad. Although Reeder recognized the darkness of his childhood, the complex layers of his personality made his own behavior too puzzling for him to understand.

Wearily, he hung up his suit and crawled into bed. He was pleased with his handling of the cheating episode. He had figured it out and negotiated a productive course of action with the school district. He looked at the volume of Proust on his night table. The trouble was remembering all those French names and characters. He couldn't keep them straight. He turned off the light and thought about Velma. As he dozed off, he savored details of his previous night with her.

CHAPTER THIRTY-NINE

By the time Reeder arrived at the administration building everyone on the promotion committee was seated. A student had detained him at the last moment, needing a signature so she could file her dissertation. He hated to be late and took his place as inconspicuously he could at the foot of the table. The Vice-Chancellor stared at him as he did so. Montclair did not like committee members arriving late.

Reeder glanced around to see who was there. Myron Seligman from economics was seated near the VC. He had missed the last two meetings because of a trip to France. During the break Reeder would have to ask him about Paris.

"We have two cases to get through today. The semester is pressing onward, and we have dozens to go before the end. Let's see if we can get these done."

Montclair ran the committee efficiently, even while allowing people to have their say. Not easy with a university committee. The first case was from the business school, an assistant professor up for promotion and tenure. Seligman presented.

"Byron Colfax is an able man. His publications are ok, his teaching good, and his service excellent. He has been assisting the governor by traveling to small towns in the state to help them develop business plans. This activity has received accolades from the Governor."

The VC, who usually did not comment during presentations, intervened.

"I thought his research was weak. Not that many publications and not in the best journals."

Committee members looked at Colfax's list of publications, which the committee secretary placed in front of them. The VC was right. Not that many.

"I guess the question is how much service to the state counts," Seligman said.

"We need excellence in either research or teaching and high quality in the other." Everyone knew Montclair was citing the criteria for promotion outlined in the faculty handbook. The problem was that service was a weak third criterion in promotion decisions. It was not given much weight. What if a candidate was excellent in service and only passable in research and teaching?

Montclair was being a stickler in his definition of the promotion criteria. Obviously, he did not think Colfax should be promoted based on service.

Reeder disagreed. "I think it is reasonable for the university to have a few people who provide direct service to the state. It helps the university image with the public. The university image is not the best, you know."

Reeder was saying what everyone knew. The university was perceived as elitist, an ivory tower that produced esoteric research, much of which amounted to nothing, often at the expense of teaching the students. Reeder thought there was some truth to this. The university did produce irrelevant research.

The university countered by claiming it was helping the state attract high tech firms and conducting research that generated business expansion. There was considerable truth in this too. Trouble was the university had no way of distinguishing socially or economically worthwhile work from that which was not. Many academics claimed it was not possible to make such distinctions since knowledge that appeared worthless today could be valuable tomorrow.

With this case the issue was stark. Colfax provided service to the state but wasn't outstanding in research or teaching. Reeder was arguing on the side of social worth. Not a popular argument in the university. It was traditional to rely on criteria derived from ones field of expertise, shutting out considerations. Reeder believed social worth should be a criterion for promotion in every case. This view was too radical for the university.

The debate on the committee went on for half an hour with the committee split. Finally, the VC called for a vote. The vote was five to four in favor of promotion. Montclair was not happy with the committee recommendation. It was within his power to reverse the recommendation but he did not like to do that. Politically, he could afford only a few reversals a year. Did he want to spend his veto on this one? The next case was also controversial. The committee was earning its keep this month. Helen Moore presented.

"Harriet Leal is an assistant professor of art up for promotion and tenure. She has an excellent teaching record, and her art is recognized by her peers. She has won six awards for her displays. Here are photos of her last art exhibit."

Since artists and musicians did not write scholarly articles, they submitted samples of their work and reviews of their performances when they came up for promotion. The promotion committee tried to make judgments about the quality of the work by examining its reception by critics. Moore passed around photos of Leal's work.

"Her latest work consists of floor carpeting that she hangs in various displays."

Frank Eagleton, from engineering, could not resist commenting as he looked at the photos of hanging carpets. "You have got to be kidding. You can't call this art! This is ridiculous!"

"Where does she get the carpets?" Seligman asked. "Does she make them?"

"No, she buys them at K-mart."

Several committee members looked at Moore.

George Harrington, from biology, spoke. "I agree with Frank. This is preposterous. The woman buys ready-made carpeting, hangs them in displays, and submits this as her work? Why not stack rolls of toilet paper?"

A witty remark for a biologist, Reeder thought. The work of artists and musicians was a problem. Committee members did not know how to assess it. Art was outside the domains of academic endeavor. Publications were what researchers produced, and it was difficult enough for a physicist to judge the work of a sociologist, let alone judge the performance of an artist. This woman's work pushed committee members to the edge.

Moore argued on the other side. "I agree it is somewhat controversial. But she has won several artistic awards for her displays. Look at the awards for her art exhibits." Moore's voice raised an octave in pitch. She was becoming defensive.

Harrington had enough. "We simply should not be judging this work for promotion. It doesn't make any sense."

The VC, who had been silent, said, "We don't have much choice. Ever since universities added departments like art and music, someone has to make decisions about promotion."

Reeder was torn. He admitted that he could not see social value in hanging floor carpets for art displays. But he backed off his criterion of social worth. He hated to think of himself as narrow-minded, voting against something he didn't understand. What happened with art and music cases was that the committee debated, sometimes heatedly, and reluctantly passed the candidates on, fearing to do harm or be seen as intolerant.

This case was more controversial than most but the result was the same. This time the candidate picked up negative votes. When the VC asked for a show of hands, the committee voted five to two to recommend promotion, with two members abstaining. It had been a combative, emotional meeting and people carried their materials out the door feeling drained.

Reeder hurried back to his office to collect his messages, papers, and luggage before he drove to the airport. He was making a quick trip to Washington and on to New York. No time to dawdle.

CHAPTER FORTY

As usual, Washington was warmer than the Midwest when he arrived. A weak winter sun was shining, glancing off monuments and buildings giving them a golden glow as the taxi passed over the Key Bridge. He could see the memorials along the tidal basin. He went directly to the National Science Foundation, lugging his bag behind him. The guard at the gate waved him through after a cursory look in the luggage.

The office was half-deserted, but Smith was waiting for him and came from behind his desk to greet him.

"Good flight?"

"Yeah, not bad. Dulles was busy, as usual. How are things going with you?"

Smith sat down in a chair facing him across a coffee table. "Not bad, not bad at all. Coffee?"

They sipped brackish coffee from white plastic cups, trying to stoke up late afternoon energy. Reeder waited for Smith to brief him.

"We seem to be in pretty decent shape," Smith said.

"What about the obligation to report to Congress about the math and science education programs across the federal government? You were over your ears in that when I last saw you."

"It's coming along ok. I assigned Jim Bishop to set it up. He's an able man. He has drawn up a list of potential blue ribbon panel members, including yourself." Smith stepped to his desk and pulled a blue folder from beneath a stack of papers. He extracted a list and handed it to Reeder.

"Here are the people we are thinking about putting on the blue ribbon panel."

Reeder glanced at the names of the fifteen people. He recognized a few from his field but not those of the scientists and mathematicians. They were from top universities.

"Impressive. Where does it stand?"

"We've sent the list to Roger Dolan, head of this directorate. He's looking it over, and we are waiting for his approval. I think he will buy the list pretty much as it is, maybe a few changes. Then we contact the people to see if they will serve."

"Great. It should be interesting."

"If things proceed we expect to have the first meeting in two months."

"What about Senator Morse?"

"She seems to have bought into the idea, at least apparently. She released the NSF money that she threatened to hold back. She does want a report on the programs soon. And we have promised her one within six months."

"Ouch! That's pretty fast."

"I know but we are hoping to get the panel in action soon. In the meantime we can collect the information the panel will need about the programs. I don't know how long I can hold her off. I have been talking to her staff about it. Roger told me that was ok. He's the one who deals with Congress."

"Sounds as if you are on track." Reeder was worried about the timeline for the panel. That was fast to expect a group that large to produce something.

"My biggest problem at the moment is with one of our contractors."

"Which one?"

"HIH. They just haven't delivered on the STAR Science evaluation, a big one, unfortunately."

"Can't you take the evaluation contract away from them for poor performance?"

"Theoretically, yes. But it isn't that easy. We have only a handful of staff members in this office, not nearly enough to do the studies ourselves. In its wisdom Congress gave us money but severely limited our staff size. We have to contract out every study rather than do it ourselves."

"There are lots of contractors around, people who would love to work on your contracts."

"Sure. But our contracting procedures are so laborious and involved that we do business with only a few firms. When we get approval to bid a contract, we have to move in thirty days. Way too fast for universities to respond to our requests."

"You got that right. Universities move in decades, not weeks."

"So we have to rely on the private market for these evaluation studies. Especially those firms that keep close to us and specialize in what we need."

"And they are all located near here?"

"Pretty much, yes. We have daily contacts with a handful of people we know can get the study done, people we can rely on."

"Sounds a little incestuous."

"A little, yes. But only a few firms can give us what we want. Naturally, they have close ties with people in our office. That's how they know what we want. We talk to them on a daily basis."

"Can't you expand the number of contractors?"

"I've tried that but to no avail. The time lines for our studies are too short. And it isn't worth it for most groups to invest resources in writing proposals to do studies that they figure they won't get anyhow. The firms we are close to are the ones who know what we want. Others don't bother to apply for the most part."

"Not a good investment for them."

"No. We are stuck with five firms who do almost all our evaluation studies."

"Shit, Kevin! Only five?"

"I am not complaining because they do good work for the most part. We are lucky to have them. But HIH has messed up this evaluation pretty bad, and I am trying to figure out what to do with it. They have done good work for us in the past."

"What did they do?"

"Not what they said they would do or were supposed to do. They didn't collect the data the way they said they would, they didn't collect the right kind of data, and they haven't provided clear-cut conclusions. Too wishy-washy."

"Well, if they are as dependent on you as you are on them, maybe they don't want to give you negative findings about your programs. It might hurt their future contracts with you."

Smith hesitated a few moments, thinking. "I guess that is a possibility. Puts me in a bind though. Roger is pressing us for firm conclusions, something he can act on, positive or negative. He doesn't want to spend all this money on evaluation and have no clear actions to take. You can see his point of view."

"Sure. But sometimes evaluations of programs turn out to be equivocal."

"I know. But you can't shell out ten million dollars for an evaluation that says 'Maybe this, maybe that.' Especially one in which the contractors didn't do what they said they would do."

"The HIH evaluation of STAR Science."

"Exactly. We may be heading into legal action on that one. I would appreciate it if you have any ideas about how to handle it. Also, I want you to talk to Bishop about the blue ribbon panel while you are here."

"Well, you'll have to give me the materials so I can see what HIH has done. And I will talk to Bishop if he's around. What about tomorrow, by the way? What do you want me to do?"

"The presentation to the governing board? Well, some members of the NSF board have asked us to enlighten them about evaluation. They see that Congress is demanding evaluation, and they don't have much information about it, though they are outstanding scientists and mathematicians. We thought you would be a good one to talk to them."

"So just some kind of introduction to evaluation?"

"Yes, though realizing this is a super sharp group. They will ask questions. Don't get too detailed. Cut to the chase."

"Ok, I'll think about what to say before tomorrow. Ten o'clock?"

"Right. In the board room. Fourth floor."

After he talked to Bishop about the blue ribbon panel, it was past six in the evening. Reeder left for his hotel, where he had not yet checked in. He needed to get something to eat, think through his presentation to the Board, and get some sleep so he had a clear head tomorrow. The traffic was thick as bureaucrats headed home in the darkness. He trudged down the busy streets rolling his bag behind him.

CHAPTER FORTY-ONE

The NSF governing board room was large and paneled, better appointed than most Washington rooms. Reeder had never been here. Fifteen people lolled about the room chatting. Reeder recognized the head of a prominent high tech firm from media appearances but no one else, other than the NSF staffers. The Board consisted of leading scientists, mathematicians, engineers, and executives from technology firms. Mostly men. Some women. A few minorities.

The meeting started with the NSF director saying a few words in greeting. NSF directors were high profile. They had to satisfy both the scientific and political communities. The director introduced the head of Smith's Directorate, Roger Dolan, who introduced Reeder, stressing his accomplishments in evaluation.

Reeder began with some history about how the evaluation field had evolved from political needs, especially the need for governments to legitimate their programs and policies. For a group like this, it was important to stress the political connections. Evaluation was not free-floating and theory-based, like the scientific disciplines. It was political in its origins, practice, and effects. Entirely too political.

"In the mid-60s, Lyndon Johnson was trying to pass his Great Society legislation. The cornerstone was the education bill that provided money to economically disadvantaged students. When the bill reached the Senate, Robert Kennedy, a powerful senator, blocked the legislation. Kennedy thought the money would be wasted by educators and not serve the interests of impoverished students."

The Johnson-Kennedy impasse and the compromise that was reached made an intriguing story. The compromise was that the educational program would be evaluated and the findings reported to Congress, the first federal mandate for evaluation. The compromise was similar to the New York agreement between the Mayor and Chancellor's offices.

With substantial money available, people from all backgrounds flooded into the new field. It was like the California gold rush. Eventually evaluations were mandated in other programs, other governments, and other countries. From there the field stumbled, bumbled, and fumbled forward. Reeder portrayed its accomplishments as modest, but promising.

He discussed methods for evaluating programs. These could be reduced to a handful. With an audience this intelligent, he didn't worry about whether they were following him. Board members picked up the ideas at once, even though the field was unfamiliar. After twenty-five minutes he paused to allow questions. Smith had cautioned him not to use all the time lecturing, aware of Reeder's occupation as a professor. Reeder didn't know whether to expect hostile comments. A Chinese American man was the first to speak.

"Would you say that evaluation is a science, Professor Reeder?"

"No, I wouldn't say that. In my understanding—which is limited—science discovers the causes of things. By contrast, evaluators determine whether something is good or bad. Often they have to deal with causes to determine good and bad. And they use research methods to do this. I would call evaluation a discipline, a new one, not a science. Values are a central, integral part. They are manifested in the evaluative criteria, which provide the basis for the evaluation."

He waited to see if anyone challenged his statement. No one spoke. If they disagreed, they were not expressing it. A distinguished, gray-haired man in his 60s raised his hand.

"As members of the NSF board we have to approve lines of research in scientific fields. We bet large sums of money on these judgments. How would you go about evaluating research endeavors?"

It was a tough question because research endeavors were especially difficult to evaluate. The outcomes of research were so far into the future.

"There are few accepted methods for evaluating research other then peer review, having experts judge the research. As you well know, NSF relies on peer review extensively by bringing in scientists to judge research proposals. Of course, the drawback of peer review is its subjectivity." Reeder suggested alternative approaches that might be worth developing.

A woman with a scarf around her neck raised her hand. "How soon will you be able to tell us whether the educational programs of the Foundation are working?"

This was another tough question, for political reasons. Educational programs had been controversial inside NSF. Many thought they did not belong in a scientific research agency. Reeder didn't know what Dolan, the head of the directorate, had told the board. He could see Dolan stir in his chair at the question. Reeder decided to leave the answer to him.

"There are a number of evaluations underway. I don't know what the timelines are. That question is better answered by the NSF staff, I think."

Dolan jumped in, glossing over a timetable. His hesitancy was understandable. He had the review of programs across the federal government beginning and a major evaluation in dispute with a contractor. He cited data that indicated that the NSF programs were successful. Reeder knew the information Dolan offered was not indicative of program success but felt he couldn't contradict him in front of the governing board.

Three more questions and time was up. Overall, the governing board seemed favorably inclined to the presentation. From Reeder's viewpoint, the session was successful in introducing them to evaluation. He had been correct to present the field as a modest enterprise fumbling its way forward. This was no group before which to display hubris.

CHAPTER FORTY-TWO

Reeder hurried back to his hotel. He had time to shower and shave. He was meeting Elizabeth for dinner. Once dressed, he took a taxi to the French restaurant on Capitol Hill where they usually met. He was half an hour early. He walked around the corner for a drink at an Irish bar that featured Guinness. He ordered a pint and thought about what might lie ahead.

He had not wanted to see Elizabeth on this trip. The last time he saw her, she raised the question of getting back together. Restarting their affair. He hadn't known what to say. He still found her attractive, his relationship with her unique. But did he want to start up with her again? She had a family to look after. It could get messy. Besides, could you go back to an old relationship that had been so intense? Both of them were different people now. Past experience suggested it was not workable. Then again, he never had a relationship like the one with her.

Whatever he thought, he didn't want to tell her no. It would hurt her feelings and damage what they shared. He also did not want to tell her about Velma. That could be developing into something serious. In the past he told Elizabeth about other women but none of those relationships had been serious. She would be jealous if she thought the new affair was. She might feel betrayed.

Reeder could see the irony of the situation. She was married with a kid, and he didn't want to tell her he might be about someone else. That was how he felt. Somehow a romantic relationship might threaten what he and Elizabeth had in the past. She would feel that way too, based on her reactions to his past love affairs.

He could lie to her about Velma but he didn't want to do that either. He didn't lie to her. Lying was not part of their relationship. They decided early to be honest with one another, wherever that might lead. The honesty led them deeper and deeper into each other. He didn't want to change that now. Perhaps the best thing was not to see her. Yet he couldn't do that. He couldn't come to Washington and not see her. That would be a slight. So he had called to say he was coming, and she wanted to have dinner with him. He was in a bind of his own making. As he finished his beer, he didn't feel good. How was he going to get through this?

He walked to the French restaurant and waited. In five minutes she arrived in a taxi. As she stepped out, he felt a surge of warmth on seeing her. The old feeling. She met him at the door and gave him a long kiss, emotional not sexual. He clasped her to him, feeling how well they fit. She was beautifully dressed as usual. How much did she pay for that coat? She held his hand behind her as the maitre d' led them to a table at the back of the room. He followed.

"So how are you? How was your presentation?"

"Good. I think it was fine. Of course, when I speak I always think that." He told her what he said and the questions the NSF board raised.

"How's your family?"

"Fabulous!" She seemed in a good mood. "John has been awarded a scholarship to the school he is attending—one of only five—which lessens the financial burden on me! The place is expensive! And I am the major bread winner in the family, as you know."

She extolled the brilliance of her son. He listened patiently, knowing how important her son's intellectual performance was. By the time she finished, the main course arrived.

"How's your New York project coming along?" He told her about the cheating scandal, careful not to mention Velma. She talked about her own work in the law firm and the difficulty of lobbying politicians on issues her firm had taken on, especially issues she didn't agree with. He listened to how she dealt with conflicts between her work and her beliefs. Perhaps she had forgotten about resuming their affair. Maybe he wouldn't have to discuss it. He was wrong.

"Have you thought about what I said last time? About us starting up again like in the old days?"

"I haven't thought much about it. I didn't know if you were serious."

"Oh, yes. I am serious. I can get away occasionally now."

"Well, I don't know. I'll have to think about it some more."

He could see tears welling up in her eyes. She guessed that he didn't want to take up with her again. This wasn't what she expected.

"You don't want to. I can see that." She didn't hide her emotions. Never did. She let them flow. "This is hurting me."

He didn't like to make her unhappy. He backed off.

"Well, I'm not saying that exactly. Now is not the right time. Maybe later. I'll think about it."

This was a half-truth. The prospect of starting up with her made him realize that he was serious about Velma. Yet he couldn't say no to Elizabeth.

"Is there someone else you are serious about?"

"Well, no, not exactly."

This wasn't even a half-truth, he knew. He was trying to extricate himself however he could without rejecting her. Being forthright would be the best course of action. Get it over with. He couldn't do it. Besides, he wasn't sure himself now.

"Well, ok. If you change your mind, let me know. I'll always love you. You know that." She placed her hand over his on the table, recovering her composure. He felt upset, agitated. They chatted for half an hour about trivial matters, neither wanting to revisit the topic. He listened, distracted by his emotions, which he tried to settle down, without success. As they parted, she kissed him on the mouth and pressed her body to him, her face into his neck. She got into a taxi and waved goodbye.

Early next morning he was still upset as he caught a taxi to the airport. Rather than return to the Midwest he was flying directly to New York to meet with the assistant Chancellor about the cheating scandal. Kepner wanted to talk about his second report, the one with the cheating allegations. Was this meeting going to be as confrontational as the one about his last report? And to see Velma. It was important that he see her now.

CHAPTER FORTY-THREE

Reeder arrived at 110 Livingston Street early. The taxi ride from LaGuardia had not taken long. He decided to go to the top floor anyhow. He could work until his appointment. He went to the assistant Chancellor's office and introduced himself to the secretary. She called Kepner to tell him Reeder was there. This time there was no waiting, though he was early.

Kepner came out of his office smiling and extending his hand.

"Good to see you."

He sounded as if he meant it. Kepner's office was smaller than the Deputy's. It looked out on an apartment building across the street. No grand view of the city skyline. He motioned to Reeder to take a chair in front of the desk while he seated himself behind it.

"Let me get Rick up here."

Kepner picked up the phone and called Cole, the evaluation director, to tell him Reeder had arrived. Kepner and Reeder chatted until Cole walked into the office five minutes later. Cole seated himself in the other chair in front of Kepner's desk.

"We really appreciate your last report and you working with us on this problem," Kepner said.

Reeder was surprised. He had written a monitoring report on the cheating on the citywide tests. He was not optimistic about how the report would be received, given the negative reception to his last report. He feared the worse.

"Your report set the right tone for us, not too accusatory nor too righteous. Gave us an opportunity to investigate to see what was happening. As you suspected, we have a problem."

Cole picked up the theme.

"I did a study, as you recommended, which identified eighteen schools that had suspicious test score gains. Most of these schools were in two subdistricts, nine in one subdistrict and eight in the other. We gathered the materials being used to prepare for the tests and examined them. Sure enough, they were keyed to the tests."

Kepner laughed.

"He means *really* keyed to the tests. There were items from the Cosmopolitan Test in the materials. No question about it." Kepner seemed happy about this news for some reason.

"The teachers were told to teach these materials weeks before the tests were given," Cole continued. "We think that is what drove up the test scores in those schools. At least that is what we suspect."

"Can you look at individual items on the tests to see if that is the case?" Reeder asked.

"We don't have the items by school. We've requested the data from the testing company. So far we have not heard from them, except that they would be happy to cooperate."

"They did say they were concerned about the publicity, how it might affect the test's reputation," Kepner said. "We assured them we would not benefit from the publicity either. There was no reason for us to make the cheating public."

"Why would they be so concerned about the cheating? They didn't do it."

"No, just bad public relations with the Cosmopolitan name attached to it. Plus advertising how easy it is to bias test results. People elsewhere might start questioning the results they had."

"Yeah, I guess that makes sense."

Cole came back to the investigation.

"We traced the curriculum materials to the consulting staffs of the subdistricts. They used the same materials in cooperation with each other. Right now, it looks as if someone in one of the subdistricts hatched the scheme. We don't know who."

"To make the schools look good?"

"Yes, the schools involved and the subdistricts too. We summarize test scores for subdistricts, as well as for schools, and compare the scores. These two subdistricts have looked good over the past few years, as you might guess. Even before the Second Chance program began. We believe this organized cheating predates the program."

"You have local superintendents over each subdistrict."

"Yes, each subdistrict has a local superintendent responsible who reports to the Chancellor."

"Were they involved?"

Regression to the Mean 153

Kepner spoke again. "We don't know frankly. This is where it gets sticky. They have benefited from their subdistricts looking good. That's for sure. Obviously, we are starting to get into legal problems here because people could be dismissed over this. We have an office of investigation for such matters. We've turned the case over to them. They have the lawyers and investigators to go about it in the right way."

"So you have turned it over to them?" Reeder could merely follow along at this point.

"Yes, now that we have established there is something wrong, we have turned the case over to them, along with the materials we collected. They are investigating it."

"When do you expect to hear from them?"

"We don't know. I guess it depends on how extensive the problem is. It's out of our hands and with this investigation office now."

"In the meantime," Cole said, "we have instructed schools to use the same test preparation materials as all the other schools. To preclude any further problems."

"You said there was another school with suspicious results that didn't fit in these two districts?"

"Yes, we don't know what happened there. Just don't know. Maybe the gains are legitimate. They are using the same preparation materials as every other school from what we can tell."

Reeder was impressed with the speed and efficiency with which the district had acted, once alerted. He could not find fault with what they had done.

"Of course, this affects your test results."

"It might. We intend analyzing test scores with the suspect schools included in the district averages and also with them out. Then we will see what difference it makes overall. We are not sure it makes that much difference to the averages. We have hundreds of schools, you know. It might average out to very little."

"Do you have any other suggestions?" Kepner asked.

"No, not at the moment. If I think of anything I'll let you know. You have done a good job of addressing the problem, from what I can see."

"We want to thank you for your help. We would not have noticed the problem without you alerting us to it."

"Part of my monitoring job," Reeder said. He glanced at Cole who was expressionless. Cole knew something was wrong before Reeder arrived on the scene.

"One more thing," Kepner said. "The city council has asked the school district to make a presentation about the Second Chance program in two weeks. We are going to present our view. The parents union, which is opposed to the program, is going to present their view. We would like you to present your own view too. That way the city council will have three views, with yours being the most impartial."

Reeder was taken by surprise. Somehow he had gone from being an enemy of the school district to a friendly helper.

"Yes, I guess I could do that."

"Also, the Chancellor wants to see you today at five. I hope that's ok."

A complete surprise.

Reeder shook hands with Kepner and Cole. He arrived ready for another confrontation with the district administrators. Instead, he was treated like a minor hero. What next?

CHAPTER FORTY-FOUR

Reeder walked around the Brooklyn neighborhood near the school district office, waiting for his appointment with the Chancellor. A block away he found a small delicatessen. He went in and ordered a pastrami sandwich. The place didn't look that clean but he was not particular. The owner was chatty. He had served the district personnel for years and had lots of stories going back to the old days when teachers got their jobs by paying the precinct committeeman three hundred dollars. He remembered when the civil reforms were pushed through.

A few minutes before five Reeder went to the Chancellor's office. It was off to itself and paneled with dark wood, out of tune with the other offices. Four large paintings hung on the walls, not bad for a public school district. Then again, they had a lot to choose from. Maybe the paintings were donated. The office was quiet. There was only Reeder and the secretary sitting at her desk.

A few minutes after five the secretary ushered him in. The Chancellor's inner office was large, considerably larger than the Deputy's, and dark. The blinds had been drawn so the room was dimly lit. There were several chairs and two couches, plus lots of open space. In the center of the room was a large oak desk and behind it the Chancellor, who greeted him as he entered. The main light was a lamp on the desk.

Chancellor Pellegrini was a large man, larger than he appeared in newspaper photos, and more athletic looking. He might have played football in high school, even in college. He was overweight now, but not as pudgy as in his photos indicated, as if he could still run two hundred yards or take out a linebacker if he had to. Pellegrini rose from his desk to shake Reeder's hand.

"Professor Reeder, good to meet you." Said without any conviction. "Please sit down."

Reeder sat in a chair facing the desk and the Chancellor retreated behind it.

"Sam and George have kept me informed about your monitoring activities on the Second Chance program. I am glad to know you have been of service to us." Pellegrini looked at Reeder.

"Let me tell you something about myself. I grew up in this city, in the Bronx, not that far from here. My parents were immigrants from Italy. Didn't speak a word of English when they arrived. And they were poor. My dad was a bartender, ran a bar. They didn't let us speak any Italian at home. It was not allowed. They wanted us to be Americans."

He paused. "Are your parents immigrants?"

"Well, no, not recently anyhow. My family has been in the country a long time. I don't know how long."

"Immigrants are different. They're anxious. My dad used to come home from work and eat by himself. My mother prepared meat for him every evening. He was the working man of the family, the breadwinner, and deserved the best food. We kids ate pasta by ourselves in another room. We were a little afraid of him actually."

Pellegrini swiveled in his desk chair. The springs of the chair groaned in response.

"I went to the public schools here because they couldn't afford the Catholic schools. They saved money for me so I could go to college. I did janitorial work part time to supplement what they gave me and lived at home. I became a teacher, a social studies teacher, right here in New York. Then a district principal, then a subdistrict superintendent. And here I am, head of the entire school system, more than a half million students."

Reeder realized this was not going to be a discussion about the Second Chance program. At least not in the usual sense. Maybe not a discussion at all.

"As head of this district I want what is best for these students. Most of them are immigrants too. And the schools let them down. We have lots of teachers out there who just don't give a damn! They put in their time, sneer at the students they have to deal with, and wait until retirement. I know what it's like! I was there!"

Suddenly, Pellegrini swiveled his chair back around to the desk and reached his arms across the desktop. "What are we going to do about it? What?" If he had been able to reach Reeder's coat lapels, he might have grabbed them. Reeder flinched involuntarily.

Nothing was stopping Pellegrini. "That's what this program is about. Setting standards that the teachers and the principals—and the kids—have to meet. That's the *only* way you can get decent performances out of them. Set the standards and hold them to it!"

Reeder was thinking this was simplistic but he was mesmerized by Pellegrini's intensity. The man had talked himself into a passion.

"So, professor...," The Chancellor's voice trailed off as he tried to remember Reeder's name but could not. "You see, professor, this is personal with me. It is not simply a job or a duty."

"Yes, I can see that." The pause had been long enough for Reeder to respond.

"We need your help on this." Pellegrini was speaking normally now, not as carried away. "I have read your reports, which Sam and George have shown me. I can't say I liked your first one very much."

He looked at Reeder. Reeder wondered what the confrontation over his first report would have been like if it had been the Chancellor rather than the Deputy. "But the second one was ok. About the cheating. You helped us locate a problem, which could have been serious. It threatened to undermine the accountability I have tried to create for the district through the tests. It would have been especially bad if word of the cheating had gotten out. Very embarrassing to the district."

Reeder tried to think of something to say but couldn't. He had thoughts but nothing appropriate to the moment. Pellegrini was too overpowering.

"I want to stress to you how important confidentiality is in this matter." The Chancellor paused to let this sink in. "You have been pledged to confidentiality as a condition of your contract, as I understand it."

"Yes, that is true. And I have followed it exactly. I send copies of my reports only to your office and the Mayor's office. Of course, I can't be responsible for what happens to them after that."

Reeder felt defensive, though he had not done anything to violate the monitoring contract.

"We'll take care of this end. I am close friends with the Mayor. I speak to him every few days, and we see eye to eye on this program and on most things." He paused to let that sink in.

Reeder didn't say anything.

"So, we understand one another, professor."

Pellegrini got up from his chair and came around the corner of his desk to shake Reeder's hand. He moved as if he were taking out a linebacker. Reeder felt uncertain. He walked out the door trying to sort out what he had just been through. His head was fuzzy, and he didn't think it was going to clear up anytime soon.

CHAPTER FORTY-FIVE

Traffic was thick as the taxi arched across Brooklyn Bridge into Manhattan. Car lights stretched in an endless stream in both directions. It was dark by the time he got to the step-down bar in the Village where he and Velma had met for a drink the first time. She was sitting at a table waiting for him when he arrived.

"Sorry, I'm late. Traffic was heavy."

"No problem. You want a glass of wine?" She motioned the waiter over.

"How did your meeting go?"

"Fine with Kepner and the evaluation director. It was all buddy-buddy. I was right about the cheating. They have a full-scale investigation underway. They were very cordial. They even want me to make a presentation to the city council."

"Well, that's good. You're out of the doghouse." She laughed.

"But then the Chancellor wanted to see me. I am still trying to figure out what that was all about."

"Oh? He is a little overpowering, isn't he?"

"Yes, a bit. I don't think I said ten words in half an hour."

"That's not unusual."

"Does the Mayor get along with him all right?"

"Oh, yes. They are friends. You haven't met the Mayor, have you? I should introduce you. I don't know who does the talking when they get together. It would be fascinating to eavesdrop. Neither one is much of a listener. Pellegrini was able to push the Second Chance program forward even though many of us opposed it as a bad idea."

"I gather the Mayor is supportive of the program."

"In the sense that the Chancellor wanted it. And it has been advantageous for the Mayor politically during his election campaign. I don't think he would care about it one way or the other personally."

"Pellegrini said he was close to the Mayor."

"Yes. In fact, I hear that Pellegrini has political ambitions outside education. He sticks close to the Mayor."

"You mean like running for office?"

"Something like that. But he has a problem. He might be a little loose with finances."

"What does that mean?"

"I don't know. Just rumors, I guess. I shouldn't repeat them."

Reeder was curious but didn't press the issue. Velma looked too delicious to talk politics all night.

After their drink they went to the tiny French restaurant for dinner again. The owners greeted them like old friends. They were the only couple this early and sat at the same table near the window where they sat the first night. Velma was wearing a black skirt and top, her long legs well displayed.

"How was your day?"

"I had a down day," she said. "This is the fourth anniversary of my sister's death. She was three years older than me."

"Oh, I am sorry to hear that. That must be tough." He should have picked up her mood before. Too busy thinking about the encounters at the school district office.

"Like a piece of me missing. Part of me that only she knew growing up with me. All the things we went through together. We had a close emotional bond even though we didn't see each other that often. She lived in San Francisco."

"I can imagine. How did she die?"

Velma hesitated a moment. "She took her own life." A long pause when neither of them spoke. She looked for a moment as if she would cry but pushed it back. There was no doubt how tough she was. This was the first time she had shown vulnerability about anything. Even when she was in bed. He was surprised she was confiding in him.

"We came from a dysfunctional family. My mother and father should never have married. But they did. Somehow the family just didn't work. Bad vibes all around. My sister and I clung to each other during the bad times and the separations."

"All families are dysfunctional to some degree, aren't they?"

"Maybe. I just know about mine. My father was one of the founders of APM."

"The defense company?"

"Yes. He was gone all the time. On the west coast, Hawaii, overseas. Even when he was home he was distant, like he wasn't there mentally. Or at least that's how it seemed to us when we were kids. He just wasn't available emotionally."

"Was he nasty?"

"No, not really. Just distant, not there. And when he was there, he dominated everything around him. Even ordered all our meals at restaurants. My mother struggled with it the best she could but she wasn't the most stable person. She had her own problems. So my sister and I clung to each other. By ourselves. The two of us."

Reeder thought about telling her about his family. But that would detract from what she wanted to tell him. Some other time. She was the one down today. It was her sister they were talking about.

"She got depressed when she got older, a lot. Somehow it didn't affect me that way. Maybe in other ways." She paused. "I haven't had great success with men, I guess."

"You're pretty successful with me."

She smiled.

"Yes, maybe. Not with my two husbands though."

Reeder was taken aback. He didn't know about the second one.

"Why did you split with the second one?"

"The last one? He was seeing someone else."

"Oh, that's tough."

"Not as bad as it sounds. I was seeing someone else too. We just weren't in sync. Ever really. I think I married him because I felt I was getting older."

"We all have our reasons, I guess. You are attracted to someone for one reason, get married for another, and stay married for yet a different reason."

She laughed.

"True, I guess, when you put it that way. Frankly, I am unsure about men, whether they find me attractive, a person they want to be with."

He found this incredible. "You are one of the most attractive women I have met in my life!"

"Yes, well, I know how men react to sexual allure. No secret there."

He could hardly argue the point. He said nothing.

"My sister went the other way. Worked at making herself unattractive."

"Did she have medical treatment?"

"Yes, she had all kinds. Drugs, psychotherapy, the works. Except electroshock. She was afraid of that. Sometimes she would be better and sometimes worse. But the depression always came back."

"So she took her own life."

"Yes, four years ago, she took her own life. Pills. Nothing I could do. When I think about her, I always wonder if there was something I could have done over the years. Something I didn't think of."

"I am sure there wasn't. Nobody can prevent these tragedies."

The discussion about her sister put them in a somber mood as they ate dinner. Velma was down mentally. He could feel it. This was the first time she had spoken about her sister. He felt sorry for her and wanted to comfort her, bring her out of her unhappiness.

By the time they finished the meal, he thought he should catch a taxi back to his hotel.

"Don't you want to come back to my place tonight?" she said as they left the restaurant.

"I don't know. How do you feel?"

"Like I want you to come back and spend the night with me."

He felt he wanted to hold her, protect her, take care of her. Show her he cared about her, not just her body. He felt himself falling, falling into her.

"Ok."

CHAPTER FORTY-SIX

Next morning at nine-thirty he caught a taxi to the office of the United Parent Federation. Months ago he promised them that he would talk to them about the Second Chance program. They were bitterly opposed to it. In a sense this visit was outside his duties, which were to oversee the evaluation. But he also thought he should listen to information outside official channels. It might give him some insights.

The office was in a side street in a low-rent neighborhood in Harlem. From the look of the place, it should have been no-rent. The taxi driver took a while to find it. Maria DiStefano, head of the staff for the three-hundred fifty thousand member union, was waiting. She was about 40, a little on the portly side.

"Professor Reeder, glad you could come. We've assembled ten parents of students to talk to you this morning about the Second Chance program, so you can see how it is affecting the children who are in it."

She led him into a barren room where ten adults were waiting, talking among themselves. They became silent when DiStefano and Reeder entered. They were Black and Hispanic. Nearly all women. He was used to interviewing people in a group but he didn't know how these people had been selected and whether they were prompted on what to say. He could be getting biased information.

On the other hand, the usual problem with minorities was that here was an Anglo man in a suit who was from some authority they didn't understand. It could be dangerous to talk to him. Some were probably illegal immigrants. It was good to have the parent union as a buffer they could feel safe behind. DiStefano was fluent in Spanish, and she acted as translator.

"Let me ask the questions," Reeder told her.

"I am here to find out what you think about the Second Chance program," he told the group. "I am not from the school district. My job is to find out how the program is doing. How have your children been reacting to it?" He wanted specific details, not broad opinions.

The first person to speak was the one man in the group rather than the women.

"My son hates being flunked," the young Latino said. "He says he is going to quit school and get a job as soon as he is old enough. He wasn't like this before. His friends all went to the next grade and he had to stay back."

Reeder knew that the chances of students dropping out of school were increased when they flunked a grade. Especially males. Especially minorities. When they got old enough, they dropped out.

"My daughter Juanita used to like school," a quiet young Latina woman said. "Now she doesn't want to go to school anymore in the morning. I can't get her to do her homework anymore."

A heavy-set Black woman spoke. "My son says the other kids in the school call him dumb, that he's in the dumb class. They tease him about it. That's not right."

"No, that's not right," Reeder said. At least he didn't have to worry about people speaking out. Each of the ten had a turn. He took notes on a pad of yellow paper.

"What do you think people think about me?" another woman in a fancy dress said. "They must think I am dumb too because my kid is in the dumb class. I'm as smart as any of them."

"It's racist is what it is," another Black woman said. "This is the school district's way of treating us as inferior!"

Reeder was not surprised to see all minorities in the room. The school district was mostly minority since whites had moved or else sent their kids to private schools. White flight. The students who failed the cut-off score were minority students.

The parents went on for an hour and a half, reciting the effects of the program on their children. The ills covered everything from vomiting before school to denial by the children that they had flunked to acceptance by them that they were not smart. Reeder recognized the kids' reactions from research. Unfortunately, politicians and school administrators never looked at research before launching reforms. They relied on their intuitions, what their colleagues elsewhere did, and mostly what would sell to the public.

After a while he excused himself. He could see the parents would go on all day, and he had enough information. He thanked them for their time and effort and DiStefano for arranging it. He chatted with her for a few moments after they left the parents.

"We are basing our evaluation on these parent reactions," she said. "And we are presenting our findings to the city council at their meeting in a few weeks."

He remembered now that the parents union was conducting its own evaluation.

"It will represent an important aspect of the program, one not included so far," he said. "I'll be at the city council meeting too, to present the views of the monitoring team. I will see you there."

A taxi was waiting to take him to LaGuardia to catch his plane. On the way out he thought about the plight of the parents and the students. What affected Reeder most were the emotional responses of the parents. Knowing the research was one thing, listening to the parents' accounts of their children's behavior was another. He knew there were parents who thought retention was beneficial. None of them was here, not surprisingly, considering the meeting was organized by the parents union.

He wondered how Chancellor Pellegrini would react to such testimony. Probably say it was from selected parents or that they were ill informed or that you had to suffer collateral damage to achieve worthwhile goals. People in Pellegrini's position rarely heard this kind of information. There should be a way of ensuring that voices like these were heard at the top. Not necessarily determine the fate of the program but at least be heard.

He knew that it was not his job to evaluate the program but to monitor the evaluation, which had been designed before he knew about the Second Chance program. By accepting the monitoring role, he had limited his authority. By focusing on test scores, the district evaluation excluded the misery these parents were experiencing. Reeder wasn't sure what he was going to do with this knowledge. He did find it disturbing.

CHAPTER FORTY-SEVEN

The weather back in the Midwest was bitterly cold, below zero, with a strong wind blowing. Bone chilling. Reeder got a ride with a neighbor to Arthur Neil's place. Neil had been on a trip to Spain for two weeks and had just returned. Reeder hoped Neil would remember that he was supposed to be the guest speaker in the evaluation class today. Neil's memory was not the best, especially when he was drinking. Reeder arrived at Neil's at nine in the morning to escort him to class. When Reeder entered, the house was filled with cigarette smoke laced with the odor of cooked bacon.

"Oh, glad you are home. I tried to call you last night but got no answer."

"I must have dozed off early from fatigue and didn't answer the phone. Jet lag."

"How was the trip to Spain?"

"Brilliant! Brilliant! One of my sterling performances if I do say so myself." Neil recounted highlights of the conference, particularly his role, while Reeder sipped a cup of instant coffee.

"I got this lovely malt whiskey in the duty-free shop in the Madrid airport. You can't find this many places, I assure you. From near my hometown. A little nip before we go to class? It will warm you up, fortify you for the day."

"I think I'll stick to my coffee. Nine o'clock in the morning is a little early for me to start drinking."

"Nonsense! Bolsters you against the weather! It's a health drink in Scotland. It's too cold to go out there this morning unprotected."

Neil poured himself a small glass from the bottle, which was one-third empty. How many had he had this morning?

"Just remember before you get into the whiskey, you are driving today. I left my car in the garage for a tune-up."

"Yes, of course. No problem. Just a little starter for the morning. Sure you won't have a nip? Warm you up. It's freezing out there."

"No, we are going to be late already."

It took ten minutes to get Neil out the door by the time he collected his cigarettes, papers, and car keys. They walked into the garage and Neil tried to unlock the car door. The door wouldn't unlock.

"What the bloody hell is wrong with this thing?" Neil went to the door on the passenger side. That side wouldn't open either.

"Maybe it's frozen up!"

He went back to the driver side again. No luck. For ten minutes he struggled to open the car doors.

"Damn! Bloody hell! Roy must have given me the wrong keys to the car. He worked on it for me while I was gone. I'll have to call him."

Neil went into the house while Reeder waited outside, shivering in the cold, knowing they would be late for class. Neil returned in a few minutes.

"I think I know what the problem was. Roy left the car keys on the hook in the kitchen. I have them now."

"I thought you had the car keys. What were you trying to open the car door with?"

"Oh, those keys must have been the keys to the hotel I stayed in Spain. Have to send them back, I guess."

"You tried to open the car door with your hotel key from Spain?"

"Yeah, didn't work."

Reeder marveled at Neil's capacity for transforming routine chores into significant hurdles. They drove to the university without further incident.

When they arrived fifteen minutes late, Reeder's class was waiting, chatting noisily, wondering where their instructor was. He gave Neil a flattering introduction, citing his early prominence in the field. Neil began by stressing how much the field had changed in twenty years. He was a great talker and his insights were provocative. This morning he was especially fluent. Was it the whiskey? After he discussed three of his major projects, he asked for questions from the students.

The thin woman from Sweden asked how he got people to read his evaluation reports and respond to them.

"One thing I used to do was put in false information deliberately. To stimulate the readers to respond to the reports to correct them."

The students were stunned. False information put into reports deliberately? Reeder wondered if this was whiskey talk. He had never heard Neil say this before. Reeder couldn't let it stand as an example for students.

"Don't you think that's going a little too far? Putting false information into the reports? Doesn't that call into question the credibility of the reports and the evaluator?"

"Well, yes. You don't want the reports to have too much authority, do you? You want to give readers a chance to have their own opinions, not be overwhelmed by the evaluator's opinions. Water down the expertise, that's my view."

This line of thinking was so strange that the students challenged Neil immediately. Was it ethical? Practical? Effective? Crazy? Neil tried answering the charges but recognized the students were indignant. Seeing how wrought up they were about what they saw as deception, Neil began to recant. Perhaps they had misunderstood him. The students weren't buying Neil's deflection.

After twenty minutes of intense questioning, Reeder changed the topic by asking Neil about his trip to Spain. His insights about Spanish culture fascinated the students, finally throwing them off the attack. The period ended and the students filed out the door.

"That was a lively session," Neil said.

"It was. They took you to task for that deliberate falsification idea. Good thing I jumped in to slow them down. They might have drawn and quartered you."

"Yes, they must have misunderstood me somehow. Maybe it's my dialect."

"Right."

CHAPTER FORTY-EIGHT

That afternoon Boyer grabbed Reeder by the upper arm as he walked down the hallway.

"Are you in town for the faculty meeting tomorrow?"

"Yeah, I'll be there. Reluctantly. Why?"

"We have an ugly situation developing where the psych people want an extra faculty position. It could be a fight."

"I thought they said they had enough people after the last go-around. Plus I thought they didn't have that many graduate students to justify more faculty."

"Right on both counts. But they have changed their minds."

Reeder knew there were few issues as likely to excite the faculty as the allocation of new positions. Unless it was salary increases, office assignments, or parking spaces. An anthropologist said there were so few indicators of status separating faculty members that they fought over trivial matters. Every group always thought that they needed more staff, a sign of their importance. More staff also lessened the teaching loads for each person.

Next day at 2 o'clock Reeder dropped what he was doing and hurried to the faculty meeting. Boyer was there early, trying to line up votes. Nearly all the faculty members were present, an indication that something was brewing. The dean began the meeting by reading bulletins from the central administration about the new parking regulations.

It was a long agenda, and discussion of positions was placed last. The dean was smart enough to anticipate that only the end of the period would stop debate. A few faculty members straggled in twenty minutes after the meeting started. The room was overheated. Edison, the elderly member of the psychology group, fell asleep. A few minutes later Ella Latowski, another psychologist, nodded off too. What was this, heredity or environment? Reeder felt like asking them when they woke up. Last person awake gets to decide the issue, Reeder thought to himself.

The dean turned to the final agenda item. "We need to consider faculty recruitment for next year. We can hire three new people, the Vice-Chancellor tells me, based on our retirements and resignations. The question is, in what area shall we hire them?"

Marv Rademacher, head of the psychology group, made a plea for his area to obtain an extra position. "The point is that we have three areas of psychology not covered by our current faculty. Our graduate program is suffering because of lack of expertise in these areas."

The problem was that you could define any discipline by innumerable areas of expertise. Like blowing up a balloon and putting dots on it, then blowing up the balloon some more and putting on more dots. There was no end to specialization. Until the balloon burst, of course.

However, this line of rebuttal was not allowed. It would expose the arbitrary way in which expertise in all the disciplines was defined. All areas would be vulnerable. Instead, Boyer resorted to material matters he could obtain agreement on.

"That may be. But how can you justify another position when you have so few graduate students and you teach so few classes?" This was striking near the heart of the matter. What Boyer dare not say was that the quality of research was also subpar for the psychology group. Everyone knew this, except members of the psychology group itself. Since national reputation was the ultimate department goal, it made no sense to allocate resources to an area that was undistinguished.

"If we had more faculty we could recruit more graduate students and increase our teaching and advising loads," Rademacher said.

It was a backward argument, one used frequently. What the argument didn't do was persuade anyone outside the group. Reeder noticed that Edison and Latowski were awake finally. He waded in to support Boyer.

"Of course, another psychology position in that area would be desirable. But with the limited resources we are given, we have to fill our most pressing needs. It seems to me that we have more pressing needs where we have large numbers of students." An equity argument was not going to carry the day, but it switched the grounds of argument to a comparative basis.

The discussion continued for half an hour, with faculty lining up to express views, mostly on the basis of who their friends and colleagues were. From the way the talk trended, psychology seemed to be losing. They would have to regroup to fight another day. The dean kept close track of the time, anxious to end the debate before it became heated and someone said something nasty. At 4 o'clock he dismissed the faculty meeting.

"Thanks for the help," Boyer said, walking down the hallway.
"Help? Hell, I was trying to keep awake."

CHAPTER FORTY-NINE

A week later Reeder was on a plane gliding into New York City again. He had left the Midwest after an afternoon meeting, and it was evening as he arrived, the towers of the skyscrapers lit for miles as the plane notched its place in the endless train of landing aircraft. He watched the lights in the sky circling the city as they waited their turn, marveling that such a complicated system could work.

During the flight he went over his notes on what to say tomorrow at the City Council meeting. The publicity given to the Second Chance program had led the City Council to request a briefing by the school district and the parent union, a way of responding to the political pressure exerted by the parents. Reeder could understand the union opposition. His interviews with parents confirmed what he feared about ill effects on some students. The district had asked Reeder to present his views, probably as a way of providing the council members with a third perspective they could use to reconcile the antagonistic parties. Not a bad move. The district didn't know what Reeder would say, but they had dealt with him enough that they knew what he thought.

After the plane landed, he waited for a taxi to Manhattan. The queue was long and the traffic slow. It was ten pm by the time he arrived at his hotel near Times Square. He checked in, unpacked his bag, and hung up his suit so it would not be wrinkled during his testimony. He called Velma to let her know he was in town. They were meeting for dinner tomorrow night.

"Good to hear your voice," she said.

"Yours too."

"I'm looking forward to seeing you. It's been only a few weeks but it seems longer than that."

"Yes, it does, doesn't it?"

"I have been thinking about you a lot."

They chatted ten minutes. He decided to have an early night so he would be clear headed tomorrow. Maybe a beer before he went to bed. He walked to a corner bar, which was deserted. He drank a beer and left. The street was nearly empty too. He walked to a newsstand at the corner to pick up a morning newspaper. The headlines of *The Village Voice* glared at him.

"CHEATING ON SCHOOL TESTS"

He bought a copy. The article was a front-page expose of the Second Chance program. The newspaper had found out about the cheating. They had gotten hold of the confidential reports he sent to the Chancellor and Mayor's offices. How had they done that? He was dismayed. He read the first page standing in the dim street light, enough to see that the paper had the full story. He hurried back to his hotel, alarmed. He knew he hadn't leaked the report. He had warned them from the beginning that keeping the reports confidential was difficult in a huge bureaucracy. Nonetheless, he might end up being blamed.

The article was a long one, the main story of the edition. He read it through, and read it again to see if he had missed anything. The reporter had the facts correct. The regression analysis bungled by the school district, the cheating scandal, excerpts from his reports criticizing the district, and interviews with parents and students about the deleterious effects of the program. The quotes from his reports were selective in picking out the most negative aspects. *The Village Voice* was taking a strong stand against the Second Chance program.

The reporter had contacted the district administrators, and there were quotes from Sam Kepner and Rick Cole defending district actions, saying that the problems were being addressed. Damage control. Nothing from Chancellor Pellegrini. He was not available for comment. Quotes from DiStefano of the parent union stating her opposition to the program.

The Village Voice was just out on the street. If the city council members didn't know this information already, they would before the hearing tomorrow. There was no need to change what he was going to say. He would answer whatever questions were addressed to him. He worried how this would play out.

CHAPTER FIFTY

Next day Reeder arrived for the city council meeting. The room was set up as a committee hearing room with a long semicircular desk for council members, a small table in front with microphones for those testifying, and fifty chairs in the back of the room for the audience, like hearings in Washington, except the room was smaller. This was the committee that dealt with education. The room was half-full.

Kepner and Cole were there when he arrived. Apparently, they were going to present for the district. Reeder walked over and shook hands, wondering what they would say about the newspaper article.

"We thought we would present first, describe the program to them, and discuss the evaluation findings. The parent union reps can go next, and you can go last," Kepner said. "Is that ok with you?"

"Sure, fine with me."

No one from the parent union was there. Five minutes before the meeting began, DiStefano walked in with two people Reeder did not know. He sat in the audience while the council members took their places, ten altogether.

Kepner presented the district view, a description of the program followed by the good outcomes the district hoped for. Cole followed with evaluation findings, some numbers, fair enough from Reeder's point of view. Council members asked questions. They seemed skeptical about the program's presumed benefits, and they had seen *The Village Voice* article. Some questions bordered on the hostile. Kepner and Cole stayed calm, not answering in the same tone of voice.

After the first round of questions, Reeder could identify which constituency individual city council members represented. An Hispanic representing the Latino community, a young White man representing the gay community, an African American representing Blacks, a liberal woman

177

representing the blue stocking constituency, and an older man in an expensive suit concerned about cost representing business interests. It was a page from a textbook on community politics.

The testimony from the parent union was next. DiStefano and her companions moved into the chairs in front of the microphone. The two people with her had conducted the union evaluation of the program. They presented findings based on a survey of parents. Reeder watched the council members during the presentation. Although they listened politely, they did not seem impressed. They knew the union was opposed, and they saw their evidence as one-sided. On the other hand, they wanted to be respectful of such a large organization. Their questions were polite but indicated doubt about the union conclusions.

It was Reeder's turn, and he moved to the table with the microphone in the center of the room. Kepner introduced him and stepped back into the audience. Council members were puzzled as to who Reeder was. He was not with the school district, and he was not with the parents union. Who was he?

The Latino council member insisted on clarifying his identity.

"You are not the evaluator of the program?"

"No, Councilman Alvarez. Dr. Rick Cole, who presented the information earlier, is head of the district evaluation office."

"And you are not with the parent union?"

"No. They just presented. The last group."

"Then what do you do?" The councilman was frustrated.

"I monitor the evaluation to see that it is done correctly. And report to the Mayor and the Chancellor's offices."

"Wait a minute! You mean we are spending thousands of dollars to evaluate this program, and then we spend even more to bring you a thousand miles from the Midwest to tell us whether the evaluation is ok?" The light was dawning on him.

"Yes, councilman, that is the role I am playing here."

"Why in God's name are we doing that?" Alvarez was angry at the complexity and cost of the monitoring.

Reeder thought about the Chancellor, the Mayor, the comptroller, the parents union, the newspapers, and the others. He answered as honestly as he could.

"Well, councilman, as far as I can tell it's because no one in New York City trusts anyone else. And you have to bring in someone from the outside for an opinion people will believe."

There was stunned silence. The entire room burst into laughter, including Councilor Alvarez and other council members. The simplicity of the answer struck them as near the truth.

After the laughter subsided, Alvarez said, "Well, you have come this far. Let's see what you have to say."

Reeder presented his view of the program, which was consistent with the district's presentation, but more cautious about the program's prospects. He indicated that the evaluation did not assess the emotional effects retention had on some students, backing the parent union assertions.

Council members listened. Reeder's voice had the calm inflection of someone who knew what he was talking about, someone with no personal interest in promoting or attacking the program. Council members recognized his perspective was as unbiased as they were likely to get. From questions that followed, it appeared they accepted Reeder's assessment.

The city council had no direct authority over the school district. That was under control of the school board, which appointed the Chancellor. However, the council's influence was significant. It would be difficult to continue a program that had substantial council opposition. What the council members heard was that the program was not accomplishing the things claimed for it and that it was too soon to tell whether it might increase test scores. So far it had not.

The council chair thanked those who testified and dismissed the hearing. Kepner seemed pleased with how the hearing had gone, though it was not all in the program's favor. He asked Reeder if he would like to have a beer. Although Reeder was meeting Velma, he thought it politic to accept.

CHAPTER FIFTY-ONE

They found a bar a few doors down the street. It was an Irish place specializing in Guinness the way it was served in Ireland. Both men ordered a pint and carried their foaming drinks to a table near the back. The bar was empty except for them and the bartender, who was watching soap operas on television.

"Cheers."

"Cheers."

They toasted each other and sipped the thick black liquid. Reeder thought the brackish taste was like nothing else, like heavy coffee or tobacco, as it settled back on the tongue. He could see why people became addicted to it when it was served right. The bartender said the gas injected in the beer made the difference in quality.

"I thought that went really well with the city council," Kepner said. "And your part was valuable. They believed what you said. They had a few doubts about our view, and maybe the union's too."

That was Reeder's perception as well. "Glad to be of help. I didn't know how the article in *The Village Voice* would affect the council."

"I didn't either but it worked out fine."

Reeder didn't know whether to bring up the subject of the newspaper article but decided he had best face it head on. He was an obvious suspect for the leak.

"By the way, I didn't have anything to do with leaking the monitoring reports to the newspaper. The first I knew of it was last night when I saw the paper on the newsstand."

Kepner grimaced and shrugged his shoulders. "Don't know what happened there. Suddenly I get a call from the reporter. I figured better to talk to him than keep silent. He already had your reports. The article didn't make the Second Chance program look good though, did it? Pellegrini won't be happy. Haven't had a chance to talk to him about it yet. He's in Washington."

"At least the city council considered other viewpoints than just the article. I wonder why the newspaper even bothered with the program. Front-page stuff."

"The paper doesn't like the Chancellor. Neither does *The Times.* They would like to get rid of him. Get a minority in the job. They have been after him for some time. He won't like the article when he sees it."

Kepner had finished his beer by the time Reeder was half done. He was a big guy who looked as if he could hold a lot.

"Another? My turn to buy, I think."

Kepner got up and walked to the bar while Reeder finished his drink. Kepner was a nice guy, Reeder thought. This was the first time they had a chance to interact socially. From their early contacts Reeder thought they might hit it off together but so far everything had been business. Antagonistic at that, given the situation.

Kepner returned with two brimming black pints. During the next glass they loosened up. The alcohol was having its effect. Halfway through the second pint, Kepner looked at Reeder.

"You met with the Chancellor on your last trip. What do you think of him?"

"Well, he is a powerful personality, no doubt about it. In fact, he is overpowering. I hardly had a chance to say anything. Maybe you need someone like that to break new ground. Someone who is charismatic and certain of his position. Someone with a strong sense of mission. Actually, though, I don't think I would like to work for him. I don't think I like him much as a person."

As soon as he said it, Reeder realized the beer was making him more open in expressing his opinions than he should be. He was in no position to be giving candid assessments of the Chancellor's personality. He was letting his success in the council meeting go to his head. He backtracked so he didn't sound too negative.

"I guess he is ok. I might like him if I knew him better. You work for him. What do you think of him?"

Kepner laughed. He was letting his guard down too.

"He is a powerful personality, no doubt about that. I met him years ago when I was in Washington with the education department, and he got me to come up here. I could see he wanted to do something for the kids. He had a sense of purpose, not just ambition. That appealed to me."

He paused to take another swig of beer.

"I haven't been disappointed in that way. He is peculiar though. Among other things, he borrows money from his staff. I never encountered that in a boss before. And I had some weird bosses in Washington, believe me. I had one boss who used to wax his legs and wear panty hose to work beneath his suit. Don't know how he could tell if he had a run!" Kepner laughed.

"What do you mean borrows money?"

"Borrows money. Here he is making way more than we are, and he borrows money from us, from all the assistant and associate Chancellors, from what I can tell."

"You mean to make ends meet until the next payday?"

"No, I mean real money. He borrowed thirty thousand dollars from me. I don't know how much he has borrowed from the others."

"Does he pay it back?"

"I don't know. I hope so. He hasn't paid me back yet. I know that. And he borrows it interest free. No interest. Like a loan between friends."

Reeder was shocked. He hadn't encountered anything quite like this.

"You're joking!"

"No, I am not joking." Kepner reached into his billfold and pulled out a crumpled piece of paper from beneath his driver's license. He showed it to Reeder.

"Here's his IOU. 'I owe you $30,000. R. Pellegrini.'"

Reeder could see the scribbled handwriting, barely legible, and Pellegrini's signature. He could hardly believe it.

"That doesn't seem right to me, borrowing money from your subordinates with no interest." It was weak understatement and he knew it.

"No, not to me either, frankly. As I say, he's a funny guy. In other ways he's great to work for. He's loyal. He'll back you up, give you credit for your work. But he has some quirks."

"Did he pressure you to borrow it?"

Kepner thought for a few seconds.

"I'm not sure. I mean, I don't think you would feel comfortable not loaning it to him when he asks. There is a kind of pressure. But it's unspoken."

"Do you think it's the power thing? That he wants to show you he has power over his subordinates, a mind game? Or does he need the money?"

"I don't know. I really don't know. Beats the hell out of me. He is certainly not into playing second fiddle to anyone. A real alpha male."

Kepner folded the slip of paper and stuck it back inside his billfold.

"I hope to hell he does repay me. I need the money. I have a daughter in journalism at Columbia and a son in pre-law at Howard. My wife is on my ass about it big time. I don't feel I can ask him for the money right now though. Another beer?"

"No, I have to go. I have to meet someone. Let's do it another time."

Reeder had heard more than he bargained for. They walked out of the bar and went separate ways.

CHAPTER FIFTY-TWO

He hurried back to his hotel, took a shower, shaved, and put on fresh clothes. He hailed a taxi outside the hotel and headed downtown to meet Velma. He could not get what Kepner said out of his mind. He thought about it all the way to the Village. What business was it of his if Pellegrini was ripping off his staff? What did that have to do with the Second Chance program and the evaluation? The evaluation was his business. Nonetheless, it bothered him. The whole thing bothered him.

He was jolted from his thoughts by the taxi running over a curb as it rounded a corner. The street was crowded, and pedestrians jumped back to keep from being hit. The taxi driver drove down the avenue fifty miles an hour. He screeched around another corner and ran over another curb. He yelled at the pedestrians.

"Lousy bastards! Stay out of my way!"

People on the street yelled back as the driver careened down the street. He seemed out of control. Reeder was alarmed and wasn't sure what to do. Was the man drugged up? He seemed erratic. In which case, no use trying to reason with him. The driver carried on a sporadic patter of conversation with Reeder when he wasn't yelling at people on the street. At least, Reeder noted, he was going in the right direction.

They arrived at the bar without hitting anyone along the way. Reeder was grateful. Although he had no control over the driver, he felt responsible. He paid the bill and tipped the man generously. He was afraid not to. The driver roared off down the street. He would be fortunate not to run over someone during his shift. Reeder shuddered.

He went down the steps to the bar. Velma was there, waiting at a side table. She stood to kiss him as he entered.

"How are you," she whispered.

"Good," he said. "At least I made it down here in one piece. I was beginning to doubt I would." He told her about the wild taxi ride. The two other couples in the bar, both about thirty years old, looked him over.

"How was the council meeting?"

"Good. It went well. My testimony went down all right, and I think the hearing was a success from the district point of view too."

"You're a little late."

"Yes, I am sorry. I had a beer after the hearing with Sam Kepner, the Assistant Chancellor."

"Oh? What was that about?"

"Mostly, just chatty. What do you know about Pellegrini's finances? It did touch on that."

"Not much. Just that his reputation in that regard is spotty. I don't know why."

Reeder didn't want to tell her what he had heard. No use implicating her in it. As the Mayor's assistant she might feel compelled to take some action. And all he had was Kepner's word that something was amiss. That and the IOU. It was outside his expertise. They chatted a while about what was said at the hearing while they drank a glass of wine.

"I wanted to come to hear you testify but figured I had best not. I'll bet you were brilliant."

"I might have been highly distracted by your legs."

She laughed. "I thought I might make you nervous."

"A seasoned public speaker like me? Not likely." They were joking easily, without worrying about how the other person was going to take it.

"By the way, summer's coming, and I have to put in a request to the Mayor's chief of staff for time off pretty soon. There's a place on the Costa del Sol, in Spain, where I go sometimes. I wonder if you would be interested in spending a week or so there in July? Or am I being too forward?"

He laughed. "I like aggressive women. Makes me feel wanted. Never been there before. Isn't it a little warm that time of year?"

"Yes, pretty warm, but not bad if you stay right on the beach, where this place is. A villa looking out over the Mediterranean. Not many British tourists eating fish and chips either."

"Sounds good. I think I would like that."

After they finished the wine they walked to the little French restaurant. Although they knew they should try some place different, they yielded to the temptation to maintain their dining tradition, brief though it had been. Doing the same things together had been established without planning. Now it was something they shared.

At the restaurant they were greeted by the man and woman running it, happy to be complicit in the romance they saw developing. Reeder ordered Dover sole, and Velma veal. They shared a bottle of wine while waiting for their food.

"I am glad you are here. I really missed you," she said.

"I missed you too. A lot. It was only a few weeks but it seems much longer."

"It seems as if we're in a world of our own when we are together. Nobody else, just us."

"That's how I feel too. A little world of our own. I wish we never had to leave it."

They looked into each other's eyes. Reeder realized they were reliving romantic clichés. Even popular love songs, trite and sentimental, were meaningful. He found himself listening as if the songs were intended for him and Velma. He felt like opening up to her, telling her about himself and wanting to find out more about her. He knew he was falling in love. And he let himself go.

After dinner, they went back to her apartment. Velma walked into the dark and turned on a small lamp. He followed her to her bedroom, where she lit a candle. Her whole body was beautifully proportioned, more voluptuous than any model. He had never seen a more appealing woman. Again, their shadows filled the walls.

CHAPTER FIFTY-THREE

Next morning Reeder caught a flight home. All the way back he puzzled over the financial scam he had discovered. He didn't know what he should do about it, or if he should do anything. It was not part of his investigation. He could hardly be responsible for every ill in a school district employing tens of thousands of people. There must be hundreds of illegal activities underway. In a sense, it was not his business what Pellegrini did with his subordinates.

On the other hand, could he let it go now that he did know something unsavory was happening? This might be a crime, even a felony. Was he concealing a felony if he didn't report it to the authorities? He could hardly ignore it, could he? He could report it. But what proof did he have? Not much. Kepner's word. Kepner might deny he said it. Furthermore, was it a crime? The Chancellor was borrowing money from his colleagues. What was wrong with that?

He could confront Pellegrini. What would that accomplish? Surely he would deny it or say there was nothing wrong. Also, it would betray the trust of Kepner, who would be chastised and possibly fired for revealing the arrangement. Kepner had not pledged him to secrecy, but a discussion over beer presumed the conversation was confidential. If he had uncovered the information in a formal interview, that would be different.

Tackling the financial deal, whatever it was, would mean pulling the plug on monitoring the evaluation. The project would be over. Didn't he owe it to the Mayor's office and the people in the program not to destroy the project? The welfare of students, tens of thousands, depended on the evaluation. He didn't want to screw that up. How did that stack up against blowing the whistle on a rip-off involving half a dozen high paid administrators? Kepner was right about one thing. If what he said was true, Pellegrini was weird.

Reeder pushed his seat back and tried to rest. The flight attendants served drinks from the pushcarts as the plane bounced along over a weather front. Reeder ignored the wine and food and tried to sleep but couldn't settle down. His mind wandered.

He thought about Velma. He knew he was getting deeply involved with a woman again. Was this a good idea? His track record with women was not good. She was sexy, no doubt about that. He remembered a line from a Graham Greene novel: why did God give us genitals if he wanted us to think clearly? Not the smartest thing to do maybe. He didn't have to get deeply involved. Just take the relationship for what it was and let it go at that. A few dinners, good sex, and chats over drinks in the big city.

But he knew he was kidding himself if he thought that was what he was doing with Velma. He was falling for her in a big way, falling in free fall. The relationship had evolved beyond the casual. He knew he needed intimacy. And occasionally he found a woman he wanted to open up to, to reveal the good, bad, and ugly.

Trouble was that in opening up, he made himself vulnerable. He had to lower his defenses to make intimate contact. And that left him vulnerable. You couldn't be hurt if you didn't open up. People couldn't get to you if you didn't let them. A hard lesson he had not forgotten. But if you wanted intimacy, sought it out, you had to open up, expose your weaknesses. There wasn't any other way.

He knew that when he did open up he could be hurt if things didn't pan out. He knew from experience. He also knew that when he felt vulnerable, he could hurt the woman as well. She could strike a sensitive spot and scare him, invoke an aggressive response as he tried to protect himself. Defending himself, he could hurt the woman by withdrawing or lashing out.

The whole thing was risky business, risky emotionally. A calculating person would say the risk was not worth it. But as rational as he was, he was not rational in this aspect of his life. Intimacy with a woman was irresistible. With it, you led a first-class life. Without it, you led a second-class life. He was pursuing it with Velma now, whatever the consequences.

CHAPTER FIFTY-FOUR

Reeder was deep in his thoughts when he was thrown off his seat into the air by a sudden drop of the aircraft. He fumbled for the seat belt and tightened it against his hips. The seat belt sign came on, and the captain announced rough weather ahead. Now you tell us, Reeder thought.

Half an hour before he had noticed huge thunderheads forming. They were beautiful, enormous columns of clouds extending thousands of feet into the atmosphere, higher than the plane. Dozens of them. He could see lightening flashing inside the cloud columns. The pilot was swinging around the thunderheads, threading his way through them. They must be too dense to squeeze through.

The flight became bumpier. Lighting and thunder flashed around the plane, and rain pelted it. He could see nothing outside the window other than the wing and the wingtip light flashing. The plane plunged into head winds and cross winds that shifted rapidly. It bounced up and down what seemed a hundred feet, jostled from side to side. Passengers were jarred from their seats. Cups clattered into the aisle. This looked bad. He felt anxious.

A drink cart crashed into the side of the food pantry. A flight attendant unbuckled herself and grabbed the brake on the cart before it could do damage, hanging on to a wall grip with one hand. She sat back in her seat and buckled herself in. She looked concerned too. A child two rows back vomited, and the smell crept through the close atmosphere of the cabin making the passengers uneasy. The plane shuddered in the winds.

The pilot came on the intercom. "We are landing in ten minutes, please buckle your seat belts. We have strong cross winds, and we expect heavy turbulence as we land."

The plane descended, yawing from side to side unsteady in the cross-winds, as if it could not get its bearings straight. They eased down through the storm clouds, still nothing visible other than rain. They were about to land, when suddenly the pilot hit full throttle on the engines and the plane surged upward sharply in a steep banking turn to the left. Silence as the passengers wondered what was happening.

A minute later the pilot's voice came over the intercom. "Sorry, folks. Ground control tells me that they have spotted two tornado clouds in the area, and we had to abort our landing."

What were they doing trying to land with tornadoes near by? A tornado would tear the plane to bits. Would they reach the ground safely? Reeder became frightened, to think maybe this could be the end of the line. The plane circled for twenty minutes, bouncing along. The passengers became deathly silent. They sat tensed in their seats against the buffeting. The plane descended again, roughly against the winds. They entered the landing approach. The plane dropped down to land. Suddenly, the pilot gave the engines full throttle again, pulling out of the landing pattern, straight up this time with all the thrust he could muster from the engines. Complete silence from the passengers.

"Sorry again, folks. We were landing and we saw a plane on the runway in our landing path where it wasn't supposed to be."

The man seated next to Reeder looked at him. "Ill tell you what, I spent twenty years in the air force, and this pilot is making me nervous."

Reeder felt panic surge from his stomach up to the center of his chest suddenly, chilling as it went. Maybe this was it. They weren't going to make it. He was helpless to do anything. Fear seized him. Then he asserted himself, forcing his fear back into himself, containing it. He felt calm flow over him, resignation. If this was the end, it was the end. That was how things worked out. No need to fear. He regained control of his feelings.

On the third try, the plane descended and touched concrete, the wheels striking firmly, spewing water off the runway. They were on the ground before Reeder could make out the shape of buildings in the rain. The release of tension inside the cabin was palpable as people breathed out.

Reeder headed to the parking lot. The wind blew the rain sideways in sheets. By the time he found his car, he was soaked, in spite of his raincoat. He drove home at thirty miles an hour, the car rocking from side to side as wind and sheets of rain lashed against it. Between the gusts he could see roiling clouds not far above ground, greenish black in color. Trees bent over nearly level with the ground before the wind gusts, then snapped back around again as the pressure shifted abruptly. Some trees lay on the ground partially uprooted from the twisting. Streets were flooding. Reeder's ears popped from the changes in air pressure.

When he arrived home, his house was dark, and he switched on a small lamp in his bedroom. He took off his clothes and hung up his suit, which was wet, especially the pant legs. Exhausted, he crawled under the sheets. He looked at the volumes of Proust on the nightstand. The marker was halfway through the last volume. Not tonight. He switched off the light.

He tossed around. Thoughts would not settle in his head. He heard the wind battering against the house and sheets of rain striking it. After what seemed a long time he fell asleep, only to wake up later in the night. He didn't know what time it was. The fluctuating wind pressure disturbed his brain. He dozed off and dreamed. When he woke before dawn, he couldn't remember the dreams, but they were not good ones.

CHAPTER FIFTY-FIVE

At his office the next day he found a message from his daughter to call her. She wanted advice. You would think she could find a better source. She must be at work. He waited until evening to return her call.

"How are you doing?"

"Terrible. I just can't find a place to live. The places are all too expensive."

"Well, you knew when you went out there that San Francisco was an expensive place to live."

"Yes, but I thought my high salary would be enough to find a place. The rents are even more expensive than I thought. Ridiculous really!"

"You can't expect to get exactly what you want just out of college."

"Dad, it's not about having a nice place! These places are terrible. Small, ugly, dirty! And expensive. I don't see how people live here."

"Well, millions do, so there must be somewhere that's livable. They can't all be millionaires."

"I don't know how they do it. Maybe rent control. They have rent control in the city. The landlord can't raise the rent until you move out and someone else moves in."

"That doesn't help someone who is new though, does it?"

"Exactly. People hang on to their apartments, especially if they have good ones. Otherwise, they would have to pay a lot more."

"Where have you been looking?"

"All over, but mostly Cow Valley and the Armory area."

"Where are they?"

"Cow Valley is not far from the Golden Gate Bridge. You can see the bridge from some places. The area has lots of shops and restaurants. That would be perfect. And not so far from work. But it's expensive. I haven't seen one bedrooms that I can afford. At least not that I would want to live in."

"What about the other area?"

"Armory is when you come in from the airport. Off the expressway on the way in. It's not as nice. Cheaper though. You can get a few rooms in an old converted house."

"Maybe you're going to have to settle for something like that starting out."

"It's such a long way from work. And there aren't that many shops around. Of course, street parking is a problem, wherever you live. And it costs a fortune to rent a parking space somewhere."

"Why don't you get a place with another woman? Double up?"

"I guess I could. I just don't like living with someone else. I would like to have some place of my own. I lived with other people all the way through college. I'd like some space of my own."

"That's understandable. I'm like that myself."

"You've got a great place! That would cost a million dollars out here!"

"Yes, but look where it is. Nowhere."

"It's not that bad!"

"You're living in one of the most desirable places in the world. San Francisco is where everyone would like to live if they could. You have to pay the price, I guess."

"Well, I can't stay here with Marcia forever. There isn't that much space."

"Has she said anything?"

"No, but there is a limit to how long you can stay with someone, even a friend."

"How's your job and social life going?"

"What social life? All the men out here are gay or married!"

"There must be some available men around!"

"I haven't met many of them."

"What have you been doing?"

"Marcia and I and a few of her friends went up to Napa over the weekend. That was fun. We toured wineries and ate in some interesting restaurants."

"Was it crowded?"

"Yeah, the road was packed, bumper to bumper. You know they only have a couple of roads up and down the valley. Of course, everything around here is crowded."

"Look, why don't I send you two thousand dollars? It might help you out."

"I can't continue to take your money. I am out on my own now."

"You can pay it back when you get ahead financially. You have a lot of start-up costs in setting up a new household."

"Don't you need the money?"

"No, I'm in good shape. You need it more than I do."

"Well, ok, if you don't need it. If you're sure."

"I'm sure. How's your work? That's why you went out there."

"The work is good. My boss has given me responsibility for two projects. So that's good."

"What about Dan?"

"He's still back there. Finishing school."

"You don't want him out there?"

"Well, no. I don't know. He's talked about coming out here but he hasn't done anything about it. I don't know."

"You don't seem that upset about it."

"Not really. What do you think about him?"

"I like him fine. Of course, it's not what I think of him that matters. It's what you think."

"Yeah, I know."

"Besides, I am the last person to offer advice on relationships. I don't have competence in the area myself."

"What have you been doing?"

"Working, traveling."

"Where have you been? Overseas?"

"No, to New York and Washington mostly."

"Well, I should go. I am doing the cooking tonight."

"Ok, I'll send you some money tomorrow. Find yourself a nice place."

"Ok, Dad. I love you."

"I love you too. Bye."

CHAPTER FIFTY-SIX

Within two days Reeder had revived from his trip. The sun was shining. Maybe spring would come this year after all. Spring would bring rain, unseasonably cold temperatures, thunderstorms, and tornadoes. At least the sun would shine over the prairies. He sat at his desk with so many things to do that he didn't know where to start. Which one first?

His phone rang. It was the Vice-Chancellor's secretary. The Vice-Chancellor wanted to see him. Now. There was no bargaining in the request. Now. What in the hell was this? People in universities didn't act like this. They set up meetings weeks in advance.

Reeder walked across campus trying to contain his concern. It was a long walk to the administration building, and it seemed longer today. He thought about what could be so urgent and flicked through the possibilities. Maybe it had to do with the case of the archeologist or another faculty promotion. Nothing made sense to command such urgency. He felt a sense of dread. Something was wrong.

He arrived at the VC's office. At least he would know soon what this was about. Montclair's office was modest in size and tastefully appointed with furniture and paintings. Reeder wondered what the paintings had cost. Montclair had a flair for the arts, even though he was a physicist, and he promoted artistic displays and performances across campus as part of his duties. In fact, for years Reeder had been avoiding accepting the VC's invitation to the Christmas concert. No more Nutcracker Suites if he could help it. One sugar plum fairy too many. He waited outside for a few moments until the secretary motioned him in. Did she give him a pitying look?

Montclair looked up and told him to sit in the chair in front of his desk. He wasn't smiling.

"I got a call from the Chancellor's office in New York yesterday afternoon. Is that the head of the New York City school district? They want us to fire you."

Reeder was taken aback. All he could manage was, "Why? For what reason?"

"Serious breach of contract. They say they have an agreement with you to monitor this evaluation for them, and the agreement contains a pledge of confidentiality. They say you violated that pledge by releasing information you had no right to."

"I never released any information to anybody."

"They say you leaked confidential information to a newspaper reporter, and it ended up in *The Village Voice*."

Reeder was dumbfounded.

"Bruce, a few days ago I was in New York. Someone leaked information to the newspaper but it wasn't me. My agreement was to send a copy of my reports to the Mayor's office and to the Chancellor's office. That's all. And that is exactly what I have done. I haven't given anyone outside those offices anything."

"Well, that's what they say. And they were not very nice about it either. Threatening a law suit against you and the university."

"I sent out two copies, Bruce. That's it. Believe me. Someone else leaked that information."

"I believe you. It doesn't sound like you. That's what I told them. You didn't do things like that. I knew you personally. Sounds like you've got yourself tangled up in some nasty politics."

"Yes, that's for sure. I'm sorry I have gotten the university into trouble with this." Reeder was feeling contrite, though he had not done anything.

"The university is not in any trouble. I called our lawyers. The New York contract is with you personally, not the university. We checked it. You didn't run it through our contracts office. It's not officially ours. Nothing they could do to us even if they wanted."

"That's true. My colleagues and I took this on as a personal consulting endeavor. It wasn't big enough to send through our contracting process." Also, the university charged sixty-five percent overhead on external contracts, which amounted to highway robbery, Reeder was thinking. Maybe this wasn't the best time to bring that up.

"Of course, even if we had been legally involved, we wouldn't have fired you. They simply don't know how universities work. Academic freedom, all that stuff. Of course, they could still sue you."

"Who was it who called?"

"What's the Chancellor's name? Pellegrini? A little bombastic, I thought. And a lawyer, whose name I forget, was also on the line. You know what they are like. I told them I would look into it and get back to them. I didn't have any idea what was going on. That's why I called you. To get your side of the story before I responded."

Reeder shook his head. "Funny thing is I was just there a few days ago and testified to the New York City Council for them. They were very appreciative. I thought everything was great between us."

"Off hand, I would say that everything is not great between you. I am going to call them back this afternoon, at least the lawyer, and tell him what the situation is from our point of view. I'll have one of our lawyers on the line too. Give one of our guys something to do to earn all that money we pay them, other than sitting on their duffs in Regents meetings. I'll let you sort out your problems with them on your own. You got yourself into this. You can get yourself out."

Reeder could see that Montclair was not angry with him. More amused than anything.

"Yeah, ok, I'll try to figure it out."

"Why don't you abandon this kind of work and do something worthwhile. You wouldn't get into these difficulties. I know you've got the brains for doing theoretical research. From knowing you personally and what your publication record is. You're a first class scholar when you want to be."

"Bruce, I want to do something useful. Not just the academic stuff that only a few people read. I want to do something that makes a difference on the ground, where people live. Not fill up journals that sit in libraries unread."

They had been over this topic before. Being a physicist, Montclair believed in academic pursuits, building theories and testing them out. Not chasing around the countryside compiling dirty data that people used politically.

"Yeah, yeah. Well, just remember that a good theory is the most practical thing around."

"I wish I had a theory to tell me how to get out of this shit."

Reeder didn't want to argue the point. He had other things on his mind. Besides, he could sense the meeting with Montclair was nearing an end. The VC was moving on to his next appointment.

"Ok. I'll take care of the New York thing." He got up to leave. Montclair got up to shake his hand goodbye.

"Stay out of trouble for a change."

"I will. Until next time."

Montclair smiled at him as Reeder left the office confused, concerned, and angry.

CHAPTER FIFTY-SEVEN

He pulled up in front of Neil's house a few minutes after six in the evening. Neil opened the door for him as he came up the walk. Thick cigarette smoke greeted Reeder as he stepped inside the door. Neil looked excited.

"Trouble, hey?"

"Yes, trouble. Big trouble. They tried to get me fired."

Neil laughed. Unusual things like this kept him from being drunk all the time, Reeder figured. Neil handed Reeder a glass of whiskey.

"The New York people?"

"Yes, the New York people. The Chancellor's office, head of the school system. Has anyone ever tried to get you fired from the university because of a project?"

Neil thought for a minute. "No, I can't say that they have. Lots of other kinds of threats though. And plenty of busted projects."

They sipped their whiskies while Reeder recalled details of his visit with Bruce Montclair that morning. Neil was amused by the whole thing.

"There wasn't any real chance he would try to dismiss you. Montclair is much tougher than that. You can't be a Vice-Chancellor in a university this size without being tough. Not a man to yield to threats. Maybe a man to make a few."

"No, I agree. I don't think there was any chance. Bruce just wanted to know what was going on. Still, I am really pissed off that they tried to get me fired. Really pissed off." Reeder's anger had not abated. He was fuming.

"I can understand that. But this is a time you need to keep your head straight. Especially now."

"I feel misled, among other things. Deceived."

Reeder told Neil about his visit with Chancellor Pellegrini, what a strange and powerful personality he was. He recounted the cheating on the tests and how the district handled it. He gave Neil a blow-by-blow account of the testimony to the city council and how *The Village Voice* exposed the program before the council hearing. Finally, he told Neil about the financial scam that Kepner had confided over drinks. Neil was the only person he had conveyed this information to. By the time Reeder finished, they were into the second whiskey. This evening, Reeder didn't seem to feel the effects of the alcohol. He was too pumped up.

"First, they ask me to testify, congratulate me, then try to get me fired."

He kept circling back to this as if he could not quite comprehend it. Or accept it.

Neil listened intently to the recounting of events, stopping Reeder to ask for clarifications occasionally.

"There is something wrong about all this," he said. "It doesn't add up."

"Well, I think they have double-crossed me. That's what it seems like to me."

"I don't know. Maybe. Or maybe there is something we don't understand."

"Well, I have to figure out what to do next."

"Sure. Of course. But it would help if you knew what was going on. There is some kind of inconsistency in the whole thing. You're the most logical person I know. The consummate rationalist. Can't you figure out what's wrong?" Neil squinted as cigarette smoke rolled up into his eyes. He made it sound like an accusation.

Reeder wasn't in an analytic mood. "I have to figure out what to do with the project and also what to do about the Chancellor's rip-off of his subordinates."

"What are you thinking?"

"I could resign, I guess. Quit the project. But that would be giving up. Maybe that's what they want me to do. So I don't want to do that. I could confront them. But it's unclear what would result from that. They could just laugh me out of the office. I could go to the authorities about Pellegrini's scam."

"With what evidence? You don't want to overplay your hand here, you know. You can't make a claim like that without evidence. I don't think that's a good idea. You could get yourself into legal trouble."

"In case you haven't been listening, I am in legal trouble. I can't take this lying down. I have to do something." It was difficult for Reeder to sit still. He stood up next to the whiskey bar as if to pour another class, then sat back down again with his glass empty. Neil grappled with the details.

"I'm wondering how the reporter got hold of the reports. How did he find out?"

"Who knows? Maybe someone in the evaluation office gave them to him."

"For what reason? Give the newspaper information that makes their evaluation look bad? Doesn't make sense."

"Who cares now? It's done and out in the open. The question is where to go from here."

"And what was Kepner's role in the firing? It sounds as if you and he are buddies. Do you think it was just the Chancellor and his Deputy?"

"I don't know really. Sam seems ok. I'm not sure. I wouldn't trust Pellegrini. That's for certain."

"What about the woman in the Mayor's office? The one you're tied up with. What's her name? Veronica?"

"Velma. I don't think she has any role in it. It was the Chancellor's office that tried to get me fired. She's in the Mayor's office. I don't think the Mayor's office had any role in this. In fact, I doubt they know about it. They probably would oppose it if they knew. They were the ones who chose me for the job to begin with."

"Yes, but they also exacted a pledge of confidentiality. And that's been blown now, by someone."

"No, I don't think they had anything to do with this latest stuff." Reeder stood up and sat back down again, not going anyplace.

"Well, I don't think getting even is the right course of action."

"It would make me feel better. I don't like being pushed around."

"I know you don't. You're the last person to try to push around. Anyone who has been around you for any period of time knows that. You react just the opposite way."

Reeder didn't respond. He sat nursing the last few drops in his glass. Brooding. Neil went on.

"Getting even might make you feel better, but where does revenge figure into the practice of evaluation? Not exactly the most noble of motives. Or the wisest." He squinted at Reeder through the slowly rising smoke.

"Maybe not, but sometimes that's all you've got."

Reeder declined Neil's offer of dinner. He walked to his car and drove home, still upset at what he saw as an assault on his person. Raw whiskey on an empty stomach did not help his mood.

CHAPTER FIFTY-EIGHT

It was two weeks before the story appeared in *The Village Voice*. "Financial Irregularities in Chancellor's Office." Front page news. Kepner was right. The paper didn't like Pellegrini. The article stated that five administrators in the Chancellor's office admitted they had loaned the Chancellor significant sums of money at zero interest rates. The article made the loans sound shady without asserting they were criminal.

Pellegrini was quoted as saying that there was nothing wrong with the transactions. Just personal loans to him from his friends. The school board was meeting to discuss the matter in private. The Mayor said it was urgent to straighten out the situation as soon as possible and that everyone should be treated fairly, including the Chancellor.

It had not taken the reporter long to break through Pellegrini's little kick-back scam. A few interviews with subordinates had been enough. The subordinates, resentful about their forced participation, were angry with Pellegrini for the way he treated them. Whether his motive had been greed or domination, his behavior had not gone down well with those he victimized. Resentment ran deep. They were quick to talk—without attribution, of course.

A day later *The New York Times* ran its article about the scam. *The Times* added that the school board had requested an investigation by the police to see if any laws had been broken. The police were responding to the request. Two days later, Pellegrini resigned, stating that he had done nothing illegal or unethical but that the confidence of the school board in him had been shaken, and it was important for the future of the New York schools that the head of the district have the full support of the public.

Deputy Chancellor George Clough resigned, too. It was unclear whether his resignation was voluntary or at board request. Nor was it clear what role Clough had in the loan scam, if any. *The Village Voice's* corresponding article was nastier, implying that Pellegrini had made a deal to get out a step ahead of the law.

A day later the school board said that there was nothing illegal in what Chancellor Pellegrini had done but that it was best for the district that he resign to escape any imputations about the district administration's integrity. The school board was dismissing any legal action they might have contemplated. Within two days, Pellegrini was appointed head of an urban reform project in Minneapolis, sponsored by the Millgram Foundation, at a salary of two hundred thousand dollars. He must have had the job in his pocket for a while. Virtue rewarded, Reeder thought.

Sam Kepner was appointed acting Chancellor until the school board decided what to do about filling the top post. The school board did not point out that the new man was African American. They didn't have to. His photo was on the front page. Kepner said that he would try to carry out the important educational reforms that had been initiated during Pellegrini's tenure. Pellegrini's vision and leadership would be difficult to match, but Kepner would do the best that he could. The city owed Pellegrini gratitude for his service to the community.

Reeder followed these events with great interest, scanning *The Times* every day for new items. His feelings were mixed. He felt Pellegrini had gotten what he deserved. Better than he deserved. Reeder had a sense of being avenged. At the same time, Reeder's own behavior was hardly exemplary. Some might argue that it was a civic duty to reveal corruption, an obligation of citizenship. And, after all, he was a professional evaluator, whose duty was to discover the truth and make it public. Revealing such information was an act of duty and conscience. Reeder knew the arguments and admired whistle-blowers in the tobacco industry.

But he had mixed feelings about himself. He felt he had done something less than admirable. He had figured that he had no way of confronting Pellegrini directly. Not with any hope of success. And he had calculated correctly that *The Village Voice* reporter had the motivation and the contacts to ferret out the scam. It was amazing how little time it had taken the reporter to do the job. How quickly he had acted on the tip. The scent led to pay dirt. Of course, much of that was Pellegrini's own doing.

Why didn't Reeder feel better? He felt he had done something ethically shady, not noble. For one thing, he had found out about the scam from Kepner, information given in confidentiality over a beer. Kepner did not expect him to convey it to others. That was a violation of personal trust. Second, he had passed the information along surreptitiously. Granted that the reporter had the resources to investigate whether the claims were true. But Reeder would have felt better if the proof had been something that he exposed in an evaluation report. That was his role, to make things public. What he had done was underhanded.

After the first article appeared in *The Village Voice*, Velma Williams called him from the Mayor's office, bubbling with the news.

"Can you believe it?" she said. "I wonder how the reporter found out about it?"

"Incredible," Reeder said. He did not have the courage to tell her he was the one who had blown the whistle, as close as he was to her. Although he had asked her about Pellegrini's financial dealings weeks ago, he never told her about the IOU scam.

How honorable was blowing the whistle to get even? It was difficult to make a case for such motives in professional evaluation. Reeder wondered what he would have done if they had not tried to get him fired. Would he have made the scam public? He didn't know.

A few days after the events in New York, Reeder was preparing for an afternoon class when his phone rang. It was the Chancellor's office in New York.

"Professor Reeder, Chancellor Kepner wants you to come to New York as soon as possible," the secretary said. Reeder remembered her from his visits to New York. First, she was the loyal secretary to Pellegrini, now to Kepner. What did she think about that? She was using her best official secretary's English.

"What does he want? Do you know?"

"I believe he wants to discuss the future of the Second Chance program with you."

What would Kepner do now? Would he kick Reeder off the project? What role did Kepner have in the attempt to have him fired? Reeder made plans to go to New York once again.

CHAPTER FIFTY-NINE

By the time the plane descended into LaGuardia, Reeder had finished his preparations. He was calmer, clearer headed than he had been for weeks. He was over the anger he felt about the attempt to fire him and over the chagrin he felt about tipping off the reporter. More or less. During the flight he had been going over the Second Chance project from the beginning and over the events of the past month, trying to piece things together. Having the pieces was not enough. You had to have the pattern to understand things. The causes.

He took a taxi directly to Brooklyn before checking into his hotel. He arrived at the Chancellor's office half an hour early. Time to spare. The secretary offered him coffee, which he accepted. A few minutes before the appointment time Sam Kepner stepped out of the Chancellor's office and greeted him as if he were an old friend.

"How are you? Good to see you. Lots of water under the bridge since the last time we met." Kepner ushered him into the Chancellor's office.

"Congratulations on your new job. You've moved up in the world."

Kepner laughed. He had changed the office around since Reeder had met Pellegrini there. It was brighter, not as gloomy. Kepner had opened up the blinds to let the light in. He had brought in a small conference table, so the office was more like a meeting room than a judge's chamber. He motioned to Reeder to sit at the table while he sat next to him at the end.

"I've also invited someone from the Mayor's office over, Velma Williams. You know her, I am sure."

"Sure do."

"I want the Mayor's office to be informed about what I am going to do. She said she would be a little late. The Mayor is having a press conference today about the racial problems in the police force and she had to be there."

Kepner shifted the tone of his voice to somber.

"I want to apologize for the effort to get you fired. I argued against it but Pellegrini wouldn't listen. He pushed forward with it anyhow. I knew it wouldn't go any place but you know how he was. Once he got an idea in his head he was difficult to dissuade. In any case, I apologize if it caused you any trouble."

"No problem," Reeder said. Kepner was referring to Pellegrini in the past tense.

The door to the office opened, and Velma was shown in by the secretary. She shook hands with both men and seated herself across the table from Reeder. She looked gorgeous in black.

Kepner turned back to Reeder. "I wanted to discuss my plans for the Second Chance program, now that I am Chancellor of the school district. To put it bluntly, I want to put it to sleep. Phase it out. I can't do that overnight. The Mayor made too big a pitch for it during his election campaign. A very successful campaign. So I have to let it fade from view gradually."

Reeder was surprised. "I didn't know you had such a low opinion of the program."

"I've never liked it, not from the beginning. It was Pellegrini's baby and we had to go along with it. You met him. You know what he was like."

"Yeah, I know what he was like."

"What do you think? Do you have any objections to phasing it out? Is there anything you see in the evaluation findings that suggests we should continue it?"

Kepner had decided what he wanted to do. But he was asking Reeder's advice before he moved on it. Reeder felt he was sincere, not simply being courteous.

"No, not really, not from my point of view. It doesn't increase test scores more than other programs, it has detrimental emotional effects on students, and it's likely to lead to more dropouts. And it's expensive. Not much to recommend it from what I can see."

He noticed that Kepner didn't bother to ask Velma her opinion.

"Of course, we want you to continue monitoring the evaluation of the program until we do phase it out. Exactly how soon we do so, I am not sure right now. There is the public relations angle to be considered."

They discussed how future monitoring reports should be handled now that the press was aware of their existence. Perhaps submit the reports to the district first, let the district react privately, then release them to the public.

"I think the point man on this should be Rick Cole from now on. He'll be your contact. As Chancellor I have too many other irons in the fire."

"Makes sense to me. I'll go see Rick right after this meeting, if he is around."

After a few amenities, the Chancellor ended the meeting. A phone call from a school board member rang through, and Kepner shifted to that call. Reeder and Velma walked out to the elevator together.

"See you tonight?" she said.

"Yes, tonight."

"The bar in the Village? Seven?"

"See you there."

She took the elevator down while he walked to Cole's office. He noticed something unusual during the meeting. Kepner had not asked Velma's opinion one time about anything. Even more unusual, he never turned to her or even looked at her once. He focused entirely on Reeder. You couldn't neglect the Mayor's assistant like that unless you knew what she was thinking. And you wouldn't ignore a woman like Velma unless you were familiar with her. Very familiar.

CHAPTER SIXTY

By the time he reached the evaluation office, Reeder had a few new ideas to work on. Fortunately, Cole was in his office and not busy.

"Professor, how are you?" He was as effusive as Kepner had been. Reeder's popularity was soaring again in the organization that had just tried to get him fired.

"Good. And you?"

"Couldn't be better. We're just now processing the data from the latest testing in the Second Chance program. Should have something for you to look at in a week maybe. Assuming we don't have any technical problems."

"Sounds good. The new Chancellor said we might talk a bit about how the monitoring would go over the next year. He said you are my contact person now."

Cole smiled. "Yes, that's what I heard. Possible my office may get an upgrade in the organizational structure too."

"Congratulations."

"It hasn't happened yet but it just might." He was a happy man, working his way up the ladder.

They chatted about how the monitoring would work during the next year, encountering no substantial differences between them. As they wound things up, Reeder broached another topic.

"You know, I was wondering about the cheating on the tests. I always had the idea that you knew about it long before I mentioned it."

Cole smiled broadly. Reeder was stroking his professional pride.

"You might say that. I picked it up in the data before you did. And although we didn't investigate formally, we were pretty sure what was going on."

"You kept it to yourself?"

"Oh, no. I told Sam. He told me to keep quiet about it for a while. He didn't know how Pellegrini would react. Then, when you came along, he said not to impede you. Let you find it out for yourself and introduce the topic. And to give you whatever help you needed. It didn't take you long to find it."

Reeder didn't tell him that he had tip-off information. Before he left the building, he asked to use a phone. Cole directed him to the next office, which was unoccupied. Reeder closed the door and called Kevin Smith at NSF headquarters in Washington. The secretary recognized his name and put him through.

"Kevin, Paul Reeder here. You have a few minutes?"

"Sure. Matter of fact, I was just thinking about you. Going to call you. We are ready to mail out the list of invitations to the blue ribbon. My boss changed a few names. People he's worked with before and didn't think would make cooperative panel members. You want to hear the list?"

"Sure. Go ahead." Reeder was in no mood to think about the panel. However, he could hardly ask Smith a favor without helping him in turn.

Smith read through the list quickly, making brief comments about panel members. Reeder half listened, his mind elsewhere.

"What do you think?"

"Well, I only know the evaluation people, who are great. But from what you have said, it sounds like a very able panel. The invitation letters go out right away?"

"Yes, today or tomorrow. The first meeting will be middle of next month. We are offering two sets of possible dates and picking the days when most people can attend."

"I'll be there. Even if I have to cancel something else."

"Good. We're counting on you. We'll do a press release during the meeting. Now, what can I do for you?"

"Have you ever run into a guy named Sam Kepner in Washington? He used to be in the Education department. High up, an assistant secretary, I think."

"Kepner? Yes, I know him. I haven't seen him for a while though. He used to head up compensatory ed, something along those lines."

"That's right."

"I think he went to New York."

"Yes, he's an administrator in the central office here."

"Why do you ask?"

"I'm working with him on a project in New York, which is where I am at the moment. A few complications have arisen. How was he to work with?"

"A good man, as I remember. Far better than most. He was around town for five or six years in the last administration. I never heard much bad about him. Is that what you mean?"

"Trustworthy?"

"Yes, I think so. As far as I know. He had good political connections on the Hill. Used to spend some time up there."

"Did you have any personal dealings with him?"

"Yes, a few. Funny you should ask. Now that you mention it, he called me to ask about you. Some time back."

"How long ago?"

"Oh, about six months maybe. He said they were considering you for an evaluation job up there that had to be done. It was important who they got. It wasn't routine."

"No, it wasn't routine."

"I told them about the work you had done for us. The high regard we hold you in here at the Foundation."

"You never mentioned it before." Reeder felt irritated.

Kevin laughed. "Hell, all the calls I get about people in this town, I wouldn't have time to do anything else if I contacted everyone. Personal contact is the life blood of this place, you know. People live and die by it."

"Did he ask about my personal qualities?"

"He did, as I remember. Wanted to know if you would be tough enough to handle a political situation. I told him, no problem. You sound a little pissed off. Should I have called you about it?"

"No, not really."

"I didn't tell him anything other than what everyone knows about you already. Those who have worked with you."

"It doesn't matter. Wouldn't have made any difference if you had called me."

"Last time I saw him, maybe about a year ago, was in New York when we launched STAR Science up there. We made a big deal out of it for the media. And I went up, along with my boss and some other people from down here."

"Politicians."

"Yes, some Congressmen and some local politicos up there too. It was a big shindig."

"Representatives from the Mayor's office."

"Yes, the Mayor, of course, and some city council members. I don't think the governor was there though. Wrong political party, I guess."

"When was this?"

"About a year ago. Before he called about you. Actually, I talked to Kepner about Washington. How things have changed down here with the new administration. He was with a woman from the Mayor's office."

"Good looking woman, dark hair, short skirt, good legs."

Smith laughed. "Yes, that's right. I can't remember her name. But I have seen her around before. Do you know her?"

"Yes, I know her. She works for the Mayor. An assistant."

"That's pretty much all I know about Kepner. I could dig up more stuff on him if you want."

"No, no, that's not necessary."

"I'm looking forward to the blue ribbon panel meeting next month. I resented having to do the review at first but I am getting fired up about it now."

"Well, I'll be there."

"Don't sound so enthusiastic!"

"Sorry, Kevin, I have some stuff on my mind right now. I'll be better when we have the meeting."

"See you then."

"Right. Thanks again for the help."

"We're counting on you to keep this panel productive and on schedule."

"I'll try my best. I hope my best is good enough. Sometimes it is and sometimes it isn't."

"You're having a bad day."

"You got that right. I am having a bad day."

CHAPTER SIXTY-ONE

The ride across Brooklyn Bridge was spectacular in the afternoon sun. Reeder looked at the top, searching for sea gulls to sweep off the spires. He admired the beauty of the construction, the massive cables girding the structure stretched taut over the high spires, forever in suspension yet held in place. He admired the bridge's complexity, its implacability. At first the structure looked simple, then complex when you looked closer. Or did it look complex at first, then simple? A man-made structure transformed into a force of nature.

He felt calm pass through him, a sense of resignation similar to when he thought his plane might crash during the thunderstorm. Sometimes things were just the way they were. Nothing you could do about them.

When he arrived at his hotel, the lobby was crowded. Spanish tourists checking in for a big week in New York. They were noisy. No one could talk like the Spanish. He waited five minutes for the elevator to take him to his room. Once there he phoned Penelope Reyes at her school. Surprisingly, he found her in her office.

"How are you, Penelope?"

"Good. I see you made use of the information I gave you about the cheating on the citywide tests."

"Yes, but I didn't give the reports to *The Village Voice*. I don't know who did that."

"Well, somebody did. And someone did a number on Pellegrini. Not that he didn't deserve it. The district will be better off without him. I never did like the Second Chance program. Him either. But I guess you know that."

"Yeah, I do. Who knows? Maybe the program won't be around much longer." He didn't want to reveal his complicity in the newspaper articles about the financial scandal.

"What can I do for you?"

"I am wondering where you got your information about the cheating on the citywide test."

"Why do you need to know that?"

"I am trying to piece some things together, that's all. Figure some stuff out."

"Is it important at this stage?"

"It's probably important only to me, Penelope." She was reluctant to reveal her source of information.

"Let's just say that someone in the administration alerted me to it, and someone else I know in the district confirmed it when I asked about it. The people can remain nameless. Is that what you want to know?"

"Sam Kepner."

"If you already knew, why are you asking me?"

"Just checking."

"You want to have lunch while you're in town? I could tell you about what the assholes in City Hall are doing now."

"Not this time. I'm on a whirlwind trip. Some urgent unfinished business. Have to get back to the university to teach classes, or what passes for teaching. Let's do it next time."

Reeder called *The Village Voice* but Morrie Angstrom, the reporter who broke the cheating and financial scam stories, wasn't in. He wouldn't be back until after four. Reeder left a message on his voice mail.

He took a walk around the Times Square neighborhood, down Broadway back around to Eighth Avenue. He needed exercise but there was no place for him to swim. He returned to his hotel room at four. It was starting to rain.

Ten minutes before 5 o'clock the phone rang.

"Morrie Angstrom returning your call." Angstrom had the hurried tone reporters always had.

"Morrie, the reason I called is I need some information."

"Shoot, and I'll see if I can help."

"In your article on the Second Chance program, you had some reports from the school district that were supposed to be confidential. Reports that I wrote. I want to know where you got them."

A long silence. "I don't think I can tell you that. You know how reporters protect their sources."

"Sure. I understand. But I have a problem only that particular information will solve. It's nothing that will be made public or passed on. I need the information to confirm some ideas I have. That's my use of it. Purely private."

He almost said to confirm a hypothesis that he had. He had been in academia too long.

"I don't know."

"Look, I did you a favor with Pellegrini. Now I need one from you. It's important to me. Personally." He was laying it on the line. Pushing the man, calling in his chips, for what they were worth.

Another long silence. "I got copies of the reports from the Mayor's office. Far as I can go."

"From Velma Williams."

"Maybe."

"Look, this is important to me."

"You might not be wrong. Of course, I had several sources of information for that piece by the time it was finished. I never rely on just one source for a major story like that. As I remember, I had union people, students, parents, and administrators from 110 Livingston Street."

"Ok, that's what I needed to know."

"Anything else? By the way, who's the investigating reporter here, you or me? You're taking on my role!"

"Maybe we should switch jobs."

"I'm not sure I could do your job."

"You wouldn't want to. Believe me. Thanks for helping out. I appreciate it."

Reeder hung up. He picked up his raincoat and caught an elevator down to the hotel bar to have a drink and think things over before he met Velma in the Village. It was taking all his effort to hold himself together emotionally. Amidst rapid Spanish chatter in the bar, he tried to sort out his emotions and what to do. It was 5 o'clock.

CHAPTER SIXTY-TWO

The taxi wound its way downtown through busy traffic. The buildings were lit up, the bridge a vague shape in the misty rain. He arrived at the step-down bar precisely at seven. She was waiting for him, as usual. He disliked himself for what he was about to do. Another side of his personality had taken over, not one that he was fond of, one that ran on track of its own.

She had redone her hair that afternoon, no doubt in anticipation of seeing him tonight. She had her legs crossed, her skirt hiked above the knee. She never looked more gorgeous. But he felt himself pulling away.

"You've redone your hair."

"I had it cut a bit. An inch. Do you like it?"

"It looks good." They ordered glasses of wine and chatted about the meeting with Kepner until he could restrain himself no longer.

"You know I talked to some people today about a few things that puzzled me."

"Oh?" She didn't like the tone of his voice. He had switched into an inquisitor mode.

"Yes, I talked to Rick Cole, the district evaluation guy, and he told me that he knew about the cheating on the tests for some time. He told Kepner about it, and Sam ordered him to keep it quiet until I entered the scene."

"Well, that's not surprising, is it? They wouldn't want a scandal like that."

"True. I also talked to Penelope Reyes. I got a tip on the cheating from her. That's how I first suspected it. You know who her source was? She said that Kepner was the source of her information."

Velma made no comment. She was expressionless.

"Then I talked to Morrie Angstrom. You know him. He's the reporter from *The Voice* who broke the story on the cheating and also the financial scam. He said you were the one who gave him my reports, the ones that were supposed to be confidential."

He waited but she was still silent.

"I guess the thing that bothered me the most today was during the meeting with you, Sam, and me. Sam never looked at you the whole time, an important and attractive woman like you. The only reason I can think he would do that was he is already familiar with you. Very familiar."

He didn't need to spell it out for her. She was a smart woman.

Velma was looking down at her wine glass, twirling it around slowly, stone-faced. She did not look at him.

His voice became tense. "Velma, what's your relationship with Sam?"

She didn't speak for several moments. This time he kept quiet too. She was going to have to say something.

"Sam and I have a relationship. We met when he was in Washington some time back. And we continued when he came to New York. He has been very supportive of me. I get down sometimes, as you know. Sam has been there for me when I needed some help."

"I'll bet he has."

She flinched but continued. "He has a gentle, caring side to him. Something I needed. That led to something else, a deeper relationship."

She looked at him now, beseeching him with her face and her voice, wanting him to understand.

"So it's been going on for years."

"Yes, for over three years. Since not long after my sister died."

"Who picked me for this monitoring job?"

"I did. But Sam knew about you from his time in Washington. You have a reputation for being tough, for not being pushed around easily."

She smiled at him, trying to soften him a little, make peace. He wasn't having any.

"So the idea was to get rid of Pellegrini?"

"No, not at first. Just to sort out the Second Chance program. Later when it became clear how awful he was, we thought he should go. There wasn't much of a plan to get rid of him. It was hazy, improvised. We just helped things along." She shrugged her shoulders.

"And so you found a tough evaluator to help things along."

She looked down and didn't respond.

"What about us? Was that part of it too?"

She looked up at him, alarmed. "No, no. That just happened between us. It just happened. In fact, Sam became jealous about it when he found out. What kind of woman do you think I am?"

"I don't know. I thought I did." He hated his response, knowing it would hurt her. It was nasty. He couldn't help himself. He was lashing out after being wounded.

He remembered that Kepner's attitude had changed toward him after he and Velma became lovers, but he didn't put the two things together. He had thought she might have lovers lurking in the background, but he never suspected Kepner.

"As I say, Sam has been very supportive when I have needed support. He has been important to me."

He didn't say anything, trying to sort through his feelings.

"You are important to me too."

He still didn't say anything. She became more alarmed.

"What are you thinking?"

He shrugged his shoulders. "Hurt. Confused. Angry. Feeling like a fool."

"What about us?" She was becoming plaintive. "My relationship with Sam didn't make any difference before you knew about it. Why should it now?"

He looked at her. "I don't know. I just don't know."

Her chin was trembling, but she didn't cry. He had never seen her cry. She always seemed contained, except when she talked about her sister.

The bartender was watching them, as was the other couple in the bar. The intense exchange had alerted the others to something wrong, even if they could not understand the words.

"I guess this is not a good night for us to have dinner together."

"No, I guess not. Not tonight."

They sat a few minutes in silence, neither venturing beyond what had been said. For fear it might get worse.

"I guess I'll go back to the hotel. I think I'll try to get an earlier flight back if I can. I have to teach some classes."

She didn't respond.

"Will you be ok?"

"I'll be all right."

"I'll be in touch with you later."

"Ok."

She remained seated at the table, looking at the floor. He got up and left. She glanced at him as he went out the door. He did not look back.

He walked down the dark street a few blocks until he found a taxi. The city seemed strange to him, a foreign place. What was he doing here with these people?

CHAPTER SIXTY-THREE

The plane lifted over the city buildings into the clouds. Reeder hardly remembered the trip back. His mind was a blur, not much there. Like a television set that had fuzzed out. There was snow on the screen and a loud buzz. He was overloaded.

By the time he reached his house hours later, he was trying to fight back with his reason, not always an effective tool against his emotions. His emotions were in control, and he struggled to grapple with them rationally. He reviewed his past history with women. Not encouraging. Not a history he would want to repeat.

He listened to his phone messages. A student, an old high school friend in town, a solicitation from a phone company. He could let those go. He looked at his mail. Bills, financial reports, journals he didn't read, and junk. Nothing interested him.

He turned on the television news, CNN at this time of night. The President was overseas, anti-American riots in the Mideast, a merger of two large banks, tornadoes in Florida. While the news was on, he fixed himself a tuna sandwich made with horseradish mustard. He wondered whether he should have eaten the food served on the plane. A pasta dish loaded with cheese. He poured himself a glass of wine, the last of the bottle, and sat down.

No matter how he tried to distract himself, Velma came back to his mind, which was in turmoil. He felt betrayed and desolate. Why had he allowed himself to become involved with her? Getting involved with women led to pain and misery. He should know that by now. He should know better than to expose his feelings this way. He ended up getting hurt.

He knew he was slipping into depression. He had been there before, and it was not easy to pull out of. The more you went down, the farther you fell. It fed on itself until you couldn't get back up. That was a bad way to go. He tried to reason with himself.

What had Velma done, after all? She had fallen for him. He did believe that. She was mixed up in something with Sam but that started long before she had met him. That was the positive way to look at it. Perhaps she had used him, especially at first. But she hadn't fallen for him then. After all, he had done some plotting of his own and he hadn't told her. Why should she tell him?

Maybe it was the blow to his ego. They had figured him out, what he would do. And they weren't far off the mark. He didn't like being manipulated. Used. That rankled him. He hadn't manipulated them. She probably would not have done what she did if she had known him well from the beginning. She seemed genuinely distressed when he left her in the bar.

He put his dishes in the dishwasher, turned off the television, and walked upstairs to the bedroom with his suit coat slung over his shoulder. He undressed and put the suit on a chair. Too much trouble to hang it up tonight. He crawled into bed and switched off the lights.

His ex-wife said that his expectations for women were too high. He expected too much. He set women up and waited for them to fail because they could not meet the standards he had in mind. When they failed, he had a reason for not committing himself to them. Had he done that here? With Velma? Was he expecting something from her that she couldn't deliver? That he could not deliver himself? He didn't know.

Would he never get it right with women? One disaster after another. He knew he was being melodramatic now. Nothing that had happened could be called a disaster. Not for anyone, even Pellegrini. It was just middle-class careers and relationships. Why make it more than it was? It was hardly of shattering significance in the scheme of things.

He lay on his back and felt a few tears trickle down his cheeks. He should be able to manage better than this. He was too mature. He felt as if someone had dealt a blow to his solar plexus. He rolled over on his side with his legs drawn up in a fetal position and put his hands to his stomach.

CHAPTER SIXTY-FOUR

Two days later Reeder arrived at Neil's in a taxi. He knew he was going to have too much to drink this evening. Neil answered the door without a glass in his hand for a change. He looked more pensive than usual.

"You look pretty serious. What's the matter, did you run out of whiskey?"

"No, no. Come in. I've got plenty. Why the taxi? Something wrong with your car again?"

"Purely precautionary."

Neil poured full glasses of whiskey as Reeder sat on the couch.

"So you are winding down the New York project?"

"Looks like it. Over the next several months anyhow."

"What do you think? A big success?"

"I have mixed feelings about it."

"Because of the woman?'

"Partly."

"Well, you did your part. You monitored the evaluation until they got it right. The program is being phased out, and it sounds as if it should be. Also, the headman is blown out of the tub, and a whole new regime installed. Sounds like one of your scorched earth evaluations. Nothing left standing. This time including yourself."

Reeder looked at him. "Don't rub it in. I'm not feeling great about it."

"You thought you were the victim of their hatchet man, and you turn out to be the hatchet man yourself. They must be surprised. You must be too."

Neil could be relentless when he got onto a moral kick. Underneath his reprobate behavior there was a Calvinist in hiding. Sometimes the moralist leaped out. Neil may have fled dour Scotland but he had not escaped entirely. Neither had those around him.

"I am afraid you may be right about that." The best way to deal with him when he started preaching was to agree. In any case, Reeder was not up to fighting about it tonight.

"Well, anyhow, it turned out fine. The program is going under, deservedly, a better man is in charge of the school district, and the kids don't have to suffer the deleterious effects of the program. It came out all right, it seems to me."

Neil was trying to make Reeder feel better, but Reeder wasn't feeling that good.

"Well, maybe. It's done anyhow. I can't change anything."

"You uncovered the truth and made it public. That's what you're supposed to do. You can't ask more of an evaluator than that."

"Maybe, but I am not too fond of the way I did it."

"I think the problem is that you got too emotionally involved. With getting even and with the woman. I warned you about revenge. What about the woman?"

"She wasn't entirely honest with me."

"That sounds a bit self-pitying. You weren't entirely honest with her either. You had your agenda, and she had hers. She did come clean with you at the end, it seems to me."

"Yeah, maybe at the end. After I forced it out."

"It seems to me she was as much a victim of events as she was the perpetrator. If you feel that strong about her, why not go back to her? She hasn't done anything that bad."

"I don't know. I just don't know." Neil had been puzzling over what to do about Velma the past few days. He was as confused as ever. He had not called her.

"That sounds a little plaintive."

"Maybe. Haven't you ever gotten emotionally involved on a project before?"

"Sure. Once I got wrapped up with a woman in a Toronto evaluation project."

"What happened?"

"Nothing good, I can assure you. She was the wife of the sponsor of the evaluation."

Reeder laughed out loud. Neil had a way of making things seem not quite so gloomy.

Neil went on. "I never did like Toronto. It's run by Scottish bankers. Too much propriety for me."

"Let me guess. She was married to a banker."

"They have a strange sense of values, bankers."

"Hard not to get involved emotionally sometimes."

"Sure. That's not the criterion to employ anyhow. Sometimes you can't help getting emotionally involved. The issue is whether you let it prevent you from doing the job. All the politics and intrigues and personal attachments are obstacles to be negotiated. Part of the job. Dealing with the emotions and politics is as much part of an evaluation as collecting data. People just pretend otherwise. To their dismay usually. Here, listen to this."

Neil went to his bookshelf and pulled down a volume of Freud. He was a big fan of Freud, though less enthusiastic since his daughter started psychoanalyzing him. He found a page with a bookmark stuck in it and read a passage.

" 'The voice of the intellect is a soft one, but it does not rest until it has gained a hearing. Ultimately, after endless rebuffs, it succeeds. This is one of the few points in which one can be optimistic about the future of mankind.' "

Neil went on. "Freud didn't have professional evaluation in mind when he wrote that. The field didn't exist back then. But it applies, doesn't it? Sometimes you have to persist against your emotions as well as the emotions of others. None of us are all that rational. Not even you."

Reeder drank another whiskey with Neil, and the conversation wandered to athletics and the chances of the university football team next season. He turned down an invitation to stay for dinner and called a taxi. He didn't feel like drinking tonight after all.

When he got home he was still melancholy. He went into his darkened house and turned on the kitchen light. He found some tuna left in a plastic container. He went upstairs and switched on his computer to check his e-mail. The usual stuff. He checked his finances. The stock market was up two percent, and bonds were down a fraction of a point. The stock market was too high. He needed to sell his stocks and take the bond yield. He had been delaying too long. He would start selling tomorrow. He headed to his bedroom.

Was every man as confused about women as he was, only just didn't admit it? Was there a connection between men who had to get to the bottom of everything and those who ended up with satisfactory relationships? Maybe love required less judgment. It was too much to think about. He was exhausted. An emotional hangover. Maybe tonight was the time to get back to Proust.